# DARK WISDOM

# DARK WISDOM

NEW TALES OF THE OLD ONES BY

GARY MYERS

EDITED AND INTRODUCED BY

ROBERT M. PRICE

MYTHOS BOOKS, LLC

POPLAR BLUFF

MISSOURI

2007

Mythos Books, LLC
351 Lake Ridge Road
Poplar Bluff
MO 63901
U. S. A.

www.mythosbooks.com

Published by Mythos Books, LLC 2007.

FIRST EDITION



ISBN 13: 978-0-9789911-3-5
ISBN 10: 0-9789911-3-3

Set in *Skinner* & *Adobe Garamond Pro.*

*Skinner* by Astigmatic One Eye.
www.astigmatic.com

*Adobe Garamond Pro* by Adobe Systems Incorporated.
www.adobe.com

Typesetting, layout and design by PAW.

# CONTENTS

# INTRODUCTION

Robert M. Price

*"That God-damned Gary Myers!"* That was the reaction of Lin Carter one afternoon when I gave him a copy of an issue of my fanzine *Crypt of Cthulhu*. It included a tale by Mr. Myers, one which Gary had long, long before sent to Lin for inclusion in his ill-fated revival of *Weird Tales*. Lin sat on it for years, and Gary was tired of waiting for it to see the light of day, so he sent it to me. Why was Lin Carter so upset? Why did it make so much difference? For the simple reason that he held Gary Myers in very high esteem, in fact as the most talented among that elite band he in his wonderful book *Lovecraft: a Look Behind the "Cthulhu Mythos"* had dubbed "the New Lovecraft Circle," namely himself, Myers, James Wade, Ramsey Campbell, Brian Lumley, and Colin Wilson. To tell you the truth, it would be beyond my critical ken to rate the relative merits of these estimable gents, and not just for fear of offending any of them. Nor will I venture to say Lin's ranking is to be accepted by lesser mortals because it was the opinion of the legendary editor of the Ballantine Adult Fantasy Series, but one must surely admit that such a judgment coming from such a source is weighty! And anyone familiar with Gary Myers's Dunsanian tales collected in his slender Arkham House volume *The House of the Worm* will have additional and ample reason to agree with Lin Carter in lavishing praise on him.

Over the years, as editor of *Crypt of Cthulhu*, I was very fortunate to successfully pester Gary Myers into penning some new Lovecraftian-Dunsanian tales such as filled his first book. They are caviar! And these should soon be collected in a book called *The Club of the Seven Dreamers*. But I also decided to press my luck and asked Gary to experiment with Cthulhu Mythos stories set in the modern world, and in a more straightforward literary style. This, too, he was willing to do, and I have published several of these in small magazines, too. But here for the first time is the Second Book of Myers, the set of those modern-age Mythos stories.

If one were to catch a single motif present in most of Gary Myers's new Mythos tales, it would have to be a certain *calling of the reader's bluff*. We readers of weird fiction, not to mention other subcultures such as the Goths, Death Metal fans, Satanists, and assorted Decadents, all pride ourselves on our gnostic-style transcendence of the ordinary world. At least we pose as being above and beyond the herd of the "mundanes" who work their jobs and seek relief from daily toil only through equally mundane pursuits like watching TV or sports events. And yet how different are we? Are we not inevitably anchored in that same dull parking lot of workaday reality? Aren't we just kidding ourselves that we are much different? There is a way to find out, or at least Gary Myers envisions there being such. Suppose the various doors located at the far ends of the corridors we enter when we go to a Goth club or some other venue of the strange were actually to open *and to lead somewhere?* That ought to separate the posers from the truly damned!

And Gary Myers shows that these doors need not even be very far down the corridors we traverse daily. If one is but in the right (that is, the *wrong*) state of mind, one may find oneself plunging through that door before one knows it. Even the most innocent amusement, even the most promising piece of modern technological convenience, may present a very ugly and dangerous side if one has the misfortune to recognize that potential. Evangelists with a bit more sophistication than their fellows often try to minimize the seeming risk of a commitment to blind faith. They will give you reasons, "evidence that demands a verdict," to convince you that the option for their religion requires not a leap of faith but rather only a step of faith. Gary Myers, evangelist of the eldritch, will, before you get very far into this collection, have persuaded you that only a step, and no great leap, will take you all the way to the Dark Side.

Robert M. Price
January, 2007

# THE WEB

Zach must have been watching for me from a window when I arrived. I had no sooner left my bike under the porch light than the front door opened and he came out to meet me.

"Hi, Zach. You said you had something to show me."

"Hi, Kevin. It's on my computer. Come on up."

He turned back inside and started upstairs to his room. By the time I caught up with him he was already sitting in front of his computer. As I came up beside him I looked at the monitor to see what all the excitement was about. But there was only a screensaver, a funnel of shooting stars.

He started talking as soon as I came in.

"I was fooling around on the Web, looking for naked chicks, bomb recipes, stuff like that. I was about to log off when a name in a link jumped out at me. I opened it up and found—this!"

He hit the space bar and the starry screensaver disappeared, revealing a page of text. It was very ordinary text, black on white like a printed book and about as exciting. Or so I thought until I began to read it.

"The *Necronomicon*?"

"Funny, that's just what *I* said. I guess you know now why I called you over tonight."

I guessed I did too. Zach and I had plenty of reasons for being friends, but our closest bond was our common interest in the stories of H. P. Lovecraft. We would spend hours at a time discussing his weird conceptions, from the titanic entities of godlike power, to the monstrous races that served and worshipped them, to the ancient and forbidden books in which their histories were preserved. We knew these books didn't exist, any more than the gods and monsters existed. But that wouldn't interfere with our enjoyment of a well-executed hoax.

I began again, this time reading aloud.

"'The *Necronomicon* of Abdul Alhazred has become well known in recent years, through the writings of Lovecraft and others, as the primary reference for the student of occult knowledge, practical magic and pre-human history. Yet the book itself has been long suppressed by the self-appointed guardians of morality and culture, to keep the rest of us in ignorance of the "dangerous" truths it contains. But "that is not dead which can eternal lie," and a hitherto unknown copy of Alhazred's great work has recently come to light outside the guarded circles of church and university. We hope to publish this complete *Necronomicon*, in a new translation, in the near future. Until then we are making available to the modern disciple of Tsathoggua, of Great Cthulhu, of Yog-Sothoth and the other Old Ones, this collection of essential spells culled from its pages, to arm him for the coming conflict between the forces of light and freedom and those of darkness and oppression.'"

That was all. Except that beneath the text were two buttons, one marked *exit* and the other *continue.*

"What is it?" I asked. "Some kind of game?"

"I don't know. I was waiting for you before going in any deeper. But now that you're here—"

He clicked on the continue button, opening a new page. This was a menu in the form of a table of contents. At least, its items looked more like chapter titles than program names. Most included Lovecraftian names like those we had read in the preface.

"Here's something that looks interesting," I said. "'To pierce the veil of Azathoth.'"

Zach clicked on the item, opening a window with a single start button under a block of text. He began to read the text aloud in his best dramatic voice.

"'Azathoth is the Greatest God, who rules all infinity from his throne at the center of chaos. His body is composed of all the bright stars of the visible universe, but his face is veiled in darkness. In the face of Azathoth, so it is written, the answers to all the great mysteries of the universe are waiting to be read. Yet only three men in the history of the world have possessed the strength of heart and clarity of mind to pierce the darkness unaided. All others must avail themselves of the power of the Mystic Eye.'

"And so on and so on," he ended, falling back into his natural voice. "The rest is just instructions for drawing this Mystic Eye thing on the wall. But I think we can ignore that part, since the computer won't know whether we draw it or not."

"Besides," I said, "your mom'll kill us if she comes home and finds us drawing pictures on her wallpaper."

He clicked on the start button. Almost at once a message box appeared on the screen:

*PARAMETERS INVALID. JOB CANCELED.*

"Parameters?" said Zach, seriously annoyed. "What parameters? We didn't give it any parameters."

"Maybe the program can't run without the Mystic Eye," I suggested.

"Yeah, right. Or maybe it's a dud. Let's go on to something else."

He backed out to the menu and we started looking for another item.

"What about this one?" he said. "'To quicken the fecundity of Shub-

Niggurath.'"

He opened the window and read:

"'Shub-Niggurath is the Mother of All, the great goddess whose teeming womb gave life to the Oldest Ones. The endless round of birth and death, of creation and destruction, is but a reflection in the material plane of the cycle of her eternal menstruation. Her avatars are as innumerable as her children. But the greatest of these is the Black Goat of the Woods, whose thousand young await rebirth in the service of the sorcerer who can quicken their mother's fecundity.'"

"I don't know about quickening fecundity," I said. "It sounds pretty gross, and not in a good way. Besides," I continued, reading over his shoulder, "it says here that the spell can only be run at the dark of the moon."

But Zach clicked on the start button anyway. Almost at once the same message box appeared on the screen:

*PARAMETERS INVALID. JOB CANCELED.*

Zach pushed himself back from the desk.

"This is bogus! Is every spell just a hokey excuse for why it doesn't work?"

But I was still studying the screen.

"Here's something we can try," I said. "'To summon a Doel.'"

"What's a Doel?"

"'What can be said of the Doels?'" I read. "'They are the parasites that suck at the hearts of suns, and the vermin that gnaw the corpses of worlds. As grave worms riddle the carrion dead to find out their deepest secrets, so the Doels bore through space and time to discover the secrets of the infinite.'

"And that's all," I ended lamely. "But at least we don't have to paint ourselves blue and offer up the blood of a virgin. We just start the program and the Doel comes."

"I'll believe it when I see it," said Zach, pulling himself up to the desk again.

For the third time he clicked on the start button. For the third time the message box appeared. But this time it contained a very different message:

*PARAMETERS VALID. JOB STARTED.*

Then the screen went blank.

"Great!" said Zach. "The damn thing hung my computer!"

"I don't think so. Listen!"

The monitor was dead, but the speakers were not. There was a low hissing noise like the start of an old-time record, and then the chant began. The chant sounded as thin and distant as an old-time record. It was so garbled and distorted that I couldn't understand a word of it. But I quickly realized that the fault wasn't with the recording, or even with the chanter. It was with the words themselves. They weren't English words, or Spanish words, or words of any language I could recognize. Some of them shouldn't have been pronounceable by any human tongue.

Zach and I looked at each other. We didn't speak, but I knew what we both were thinking. The chant was unintelligible. It was indescribable. It was everything a Lovecraftian incantation should be. But it wasn't very interesting. Surely there must be more to the game than this?

There was. Now the chant was accompanied by a vibration, a sort of low rumble that I felt more than heard. At first it was so faint that I could almost believe I was imagining it. But the chant grew louder as it went on, and the accompanying vibration grew stronger, until there could be no doubt that it was real. Was the vibration part of the chant? Or was the room around us vibrating in sympathy with it? I couldn't tell. But the vibration gave no sign of ending anytime soon. It only grew stronger the louder the chant became. And the chant was painfully loud already.

Then things really started to happen. The room lurched under me, throwing me violently to the floor. The lights went out at the same time, plunging us into darkness. And with the darkness came a violent crash, loud enough to drown out even the sound of the chant.

When the shaking and crashing were over and only the chant remained, I raised my head and looked around me. The room was less dark than I'd thought, with the computer screen still glowing faintly from the top of the desk. Zach was kneeling in its light beside his toppled chair, holding onto the desk for dear life. He looked over his shoulder at me with an almost comical expression of terror on his pale face. I wondered how I could see his face so clearly when all the light was behind it. Then I realized that all the light wasn't behind it. Some of it was behind me.

But I found more than the light when I turned my head. The violent shock had partly collapsed the wooden floor. Now it slanted downward toward the center of the room, tilting the remaining furniture crazily. Most of the furniture was gone. It had disappeared down a ragged hole about six feet across which now opened in the middle of the floor. And it was from this hole that the cold gray light was coming.

"Kevin, are you all right? Kevin, what is it?"

"I'm all right, Zach," I answered. But I didn't feel all right. There was something about the light in the hole that frightened me more than the darkness, the noise and the devastation put together. These were subject to natural explanations, but the light I couldn't explain at all. I was afraid to see what might be making it. But I was more afraid to turn away without seeing. I dragged myself to the broken edge and looked down.

Once Zach and I had played with the idea that Lovecraft's gods and

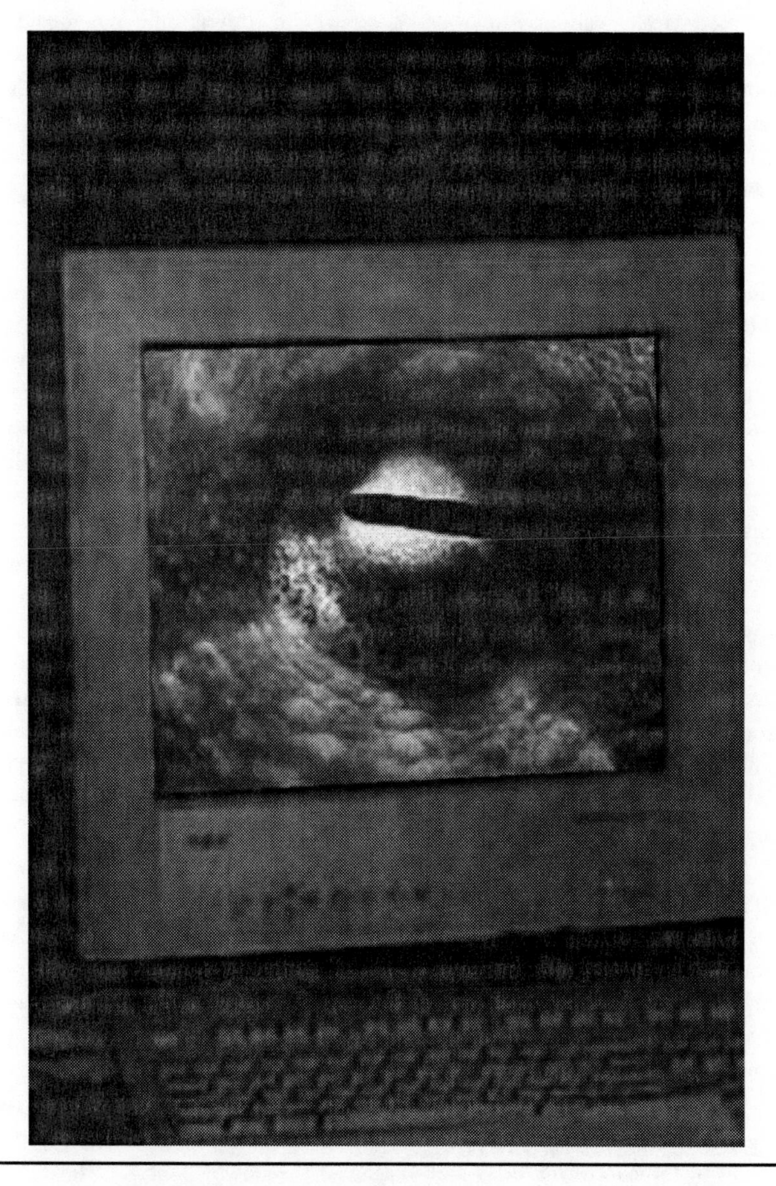

*We knew at the time it was only a game. But what if it wasn't? What if pursuing our fantasy had led us to something like the truth? What if the* Necronomicon *was real, and real cultists had published parts of it on the Web, to assist their fellow cultists or ensnare poor innocents like Zach and me? Was Zach's computer calling a real Doel to us now?*

monsters really existed, and that Lovecraft himself was only the medium through which they made their existence known. We knew at the time it was only a game. But what if it wasn't? What if pursuing our fantasy had led us to something like the truth? What if the *Necronomicon* was real, and real cultists had published parts of it on the Web, to assist their fellow cultists or ensnare poor innocents like Zach and me? Was Zach's computer calling a real Doel to us now?

The hole went straight through the floor to the living room beneath. The floor of the lower room was half buried under the wreckage of the upper one. And out of the wreckage, directly under the hole, the hideous thing was rising. Most of it was still buried, so I couldn't see its shape. But what I could see was huge and pale and coldly luminous. It was mostly a mouth, but a mouth as big and round as the rim of a hot tub, and as bottomless as a well. It glowed inside as well as out. The mouth was empty of teeth and tongue, but the throat was full of downward-pointing spines to keep anything that went in that way from coming out again. And this was what the thundering chant was calling!

"Zach! Shut it off!" I yelled. "For God's sake, shut it off!" And I threw myself back from the edge of the hole and scrambled toward him on my hands and knees. He hadn't seen what I had seen, but the tone of my voice alone was enough to rouse him into action. "I'll shut it off," he yelled back, then reached for the computer's power switch and snapped it to the off position. The chant faltered in response, but almost immediately it started back up again. "Shut off, damn you! Shut off!" Zach screamed, snapping the switch again and again. But it had even less effect than before.

I looked back over my shoulder at the ragged hole. The light above it was brighter now, showing that the glowing thing was getting closer. There must be some way to stop it. Maybe the switch was shorted out so that the power couldn't be turned off. But even a shorted computer couldn't run with no power at all. Pushing Zach out of the way, I reached under the desk and yanked the power cord out of the wall. Again the chant faltered, and again it came back stronger than ever.

I stared at the heavy cord in my hand. How was this possible? Where was the power coming from? Or if the computer was running without power, how could we hope to turn it off? I looked again at the glowing hole. The light was very bright now. In another moment that terrible mouth would be coming through the floor. But there was one thing left to try. I pulled the desk away from the wall and pushed it with all my strength toward the hole.

The desk moved with gathering speed across the slanting floor. It rolled down to the broken edge and dropped quickly over it, taking the computer with it. I heard the components crash together inside that gaping mouth. I heard the chant rise above the noise, only to fall away again as the speakers tumbled deeper and deeper into that bottomless throat. And suddenly there was no more chant. There was only silence and the cold gray light fading into darkness.

Minutes later I slid on my belly to the broken edge. I looked over it timidly, afraid of what I might see. But the monster was gone. In its place was only a circular hole, a cylindrical well plunging down and down to the center of the earth. For a moment I thought I saw a faint light glowing in its lower depths. But it faded out so quickly that I couldn't be sure.

Zach had slid down next to me and was looking over the edge with me. Now he turned to me and said in an awed whisper:

"It was real, wasn't it, Kevin?"

"Yeah, Zach, it was real."

"What happened to it? Why did it go away?"

"I don't know. Maybe it had to answer the call no matter where it came from. Even if it came from the center of the earth."

"But if Doels are real, what about the other things in the *Necronomicon*? Are they real too? Kevin, are you thinking what I'm thinking?"

"I'm way ahead of you! We've got to get back on the Web!"

# SLUGS

As soon as Jake turned the corner he knew it was a mistake. He had run into a well-lit street between high walls that did not offer even a doorway for cover. Then he saw the open manhole with its round lid lying beside it. He threw himself down it an instant before the cops turned the corner after him. There was still a danger that they would see him there, clinging to the iron rungs just inches below the pavement. But their running footsteps thundered past and away into the distance, leaving him free to catch his breath and congratulate himself on his escape.

But maybe it was still a little early for self-congratulation. The cops would not stop looking for him just because they had lost him. The streets would not be safe for him for hours. Now that he was down here he had better plan on staying awhile. But he had better do it lower down, in the hidden depths of the sewer.

The place was probably more of a storm drain than a sewer, but that made little difference to Jake. It was everything a well-appointed sewer should be: dank, dark and evil-smelling, with a shallow stream of cold black water creeping in a channel along the floor. At least the channel had a walkway on either side to help him keep his feet dry. But the walkway forced him to hug the wall, and that was wet and slimy. Still, he must not hold back on that account. When the cops failed to find him in the street they would probably return to the manhole, so he had better put some distance between himself and it. Of course he could not go more than couple of yards before coming up against total darkness. But the darkness would help to cover his retreat, and as long as he followed a straight path out he should be able to find his way back again.

Besides, there was every chance that he would not need to find his way back. The manhole was not the only way out. He had seen too many iron covers in the streets to imagine that. There were not enough cops in the whole city to watch all of them. Sooner or later he must find one, a back door to let him out where the cops were not looking for him. Or even if he missed them all, sooner or later he must find his way down to the nearby ocean.

He hoped he would not have to go that far. He had only been here for a good five minutes, and already the place was starting to get on his nerves. The darkness and dampness were the worst, but they were not everything. There were also the smells. Mostly they were the smells of stale water and the nameless filth it had washed down from the streets. But there was another smell running under these, a heavy animal smell that was worse than the

*But maybe it was still a little early for self-congratulation. The cops would not stop looking for him just because they had lost him. The streets would not be safe for him for hours. Now that he was down here he had better plan on staying awhile. But he had better do it lower down, in the hidden depths of the sewer.*

others because it suggested that Jake was not alone down here. But it was probably just a dead cat.

Presently he noticed a dim light in the darkness a little way ahead of him. A moment later he had followed it to its source, a shallow cul-de-sac opening upward to the level of the street, where an electric lamp shone like the moon through the bars of an iron grate. Was this a way out? Maybe it was, but only if he could reach it.

There was no ladder under the grate. There was, however, a low mound rising beneath it, a collection of bricks and other loose rubble arranged in a sort of primitive altar maybe three feet high by four across the base. It did not look very stable, but it should be stable enough to serve as a platform from which to stage his assault on the grate. But first he would have to take down the thing he found sitting on top of it.

He picked it up and examined it. It was a statue of some kind, a statuette really since it was no more than nine inches tall. It was hard to make out in the dim light, but it seemed to be the stone figure of a winged and bearded man crouched on a block-like pedestal. What was it doing here? Maybe some neighborhood kids had made this place their secret fort. That would explain the altar and the open manhole. But it would not explain the statuette. Even in the dimness he could see that it was no common object.

But there would be plenty of time to consider this question after he tried the grate. Setting the statuette aside, he pulled himself up into its old position on top of the altar. He rose to his feet and extended his arms as high overhead as they would go. But the grate stayed out of reach.

Just then a sound came to him from the darkness farther up the tunnel. "Who's there?" he said aloud, and immediately felt foolish for having said it. Who *could* be there? It was only the natural sounds of the sewer: a liquid bubbling followed by a gaseous hiss. But the animal smell was getting noticeably stronger.

Suddenly he had had enough. He would rather take his chances with the cops in the street than stay down here a minute longer. He jumped down from the altar and started back toward the open manhole. But he took the statuette with him. It would teach its owners to be more careful of their property.

There was no one waiting for him in the street above, and no one to meet him on the short walk back to his cheap residential hotel. That was good, because anyone who saw him would be sure to remember him, wet and slimy and carrying a bulky object wrapped in his jacket. He ran a greater risk in the hotel lobby, but his luck held even there. There was no one to see him but the clerk behind the desk, and he was too engrossed in the magazine he was reading to pay any attention to Jake. After that it was comparatively easy to climb the stairs to his room on the third floor. And when he had locked and chained himself in he considered himself home free.

Well, maybe not yet. He still had to deal with the aftermath of the night's adventure. He took off his soiled clothes and left them to soak in the bathroom sink. He soaped and scoured himself under a scalding shower. Then he threw himself down on the unmade bed with his head propped up by the pillows, turned on the TV across the room and started flipping through the channels. He told himself that he was too anxious, that the story was not important enough to get much coverage, that in any case it was impossible for it to be covered so soon. But it was hard to believe that about what was for him the most important story in the world.

It had not started out that way. The early stages of the break-in had gone as smoothly as any job Jake had ever been involved in. They had gone so smoothly that Jake had had no idea that anything was wrong until the moment the office door burst open beside him and the cop came through it waving his gun around. Even then the situation had not seemed beyond repair. The cop was alone, and so focused on the flashlight that Jake had left burning in the middle of the floor that he forgot to look behind him. And the crowbar was already in Jake's hand. But such a remedy was only effective if the fallen man was truly alone, and this one had brought his friends along. Jake had managed to get out ahead of them, but not far enough to prevent them from catching sight of him and chasing him across half the city before he lost them in the sewer. At least there was not much danger of their picking up his trail again anytime soon. But that did not change the fact that he had come back to this stinking hellhole with nothing to show for his trouble.

But that was not quite right. He *did* have something to show: the statuette from the sewer. He looked at the thing where he had left it, crouching under the electric lamp on the table at his bedside. It was a funny sort of object to have found in a sewer. But he could not imagine anyone voluntarily keeping it anywhere else. It was certainly skillfully made. But the skill of its making only increased its ugliness by heightening the realism of its portrayal. The warm glow of the shaded lamp brought out details that Jake had missed in the darkness, details which were grotesque by themselves, but which came together to create a powerful impression of brutality and evil. The nude body was flabby and scaly, with clawed hands and feet as well as bat-like wings. And it appeared that what Jake had taken for a beard was really a cluster of worm-like tentacles sprouting from a face whose only feature it was.

Jake reached over and switched off the light. He had seen enough of the thing for one night. And after tomorrow he would never have to see it again. Ugly or not, an object so unusual must be worth a lot of money. He would take it down to Manny Green's and see what the pawnbroker would give for it.

Jake never visited Manny's place without wondering how it managed to stay open. Even in broad daylight it did not look inviting. The entrance was small and dark, the door set deep between two grimy windows loaded with the kind of junk that most people would pay to have hauled away. And behind the door was not much better. It just continued on the same plan for twenty feet or more, with floor cases and wall displays filling in for the windows on either side, and the pawnbroker's cage across the back. There were no customers today, just as there had been none on the dozen or so other days that Jake was here. There were only Jake and the pawnbroker himself.

"Hello, Jake. What have you got for me today?"

"Something special, Manny. A regular *objet d'art*."

He unwrapped the statuette and pushed it across the counter. The old man picked it up and examined it closely, turning it over and over in his slightly trembling hands.

"Where'd you get this?" he asked.

"My uncle died and left it to me."

The pawnbroker frowned and shook his head. "It's been a bad year for uncles."

"I bet you never saw anything like *that* before."

"You lose. I saw one just like this a long time ago, in Prague after the war. It represents Cthulhu, a kind of devil or monster once widely worshipped as a god. Ugly, isn't he? He isn't nearly as ugly as his cult used to be. For sex orgies, blood sacrifices, torture and murder it surpassed anything that has been seen before or since. I believe he still has a following among certain primitive peoples in the far corners of the world. But most of his worshippers aren't human."

"Aren't human? What are they, animals?"

The pawnbroker looked from the statuette to its owner. "Why not? The world's a big place, Jake. Big enough to contain all kinds of things *you've* never seen or heard of. Intelligence isn't limited to human beings. Neither is depravity. So why not animals?"

But Jake refused to be distracted. "A thing like that must be pretty valuable."

"To the right buyer maybe. Not to me. People don't come into a place like this to buy statues, especially not statues as ugly as this one. Maybe I can find a buyer for it, but only if I can keep the price down."

He put the statuette back on the counter.

"I'll give you twenty bucks."

Jake did not try to argue with Manny. He would have taken a lot less to be rid of the statuette. Its ugliness aside, it was the last thing tying him to the nightmare of the night before. Now that it was gone, he felt as if an enormous weight had been lifted from his shoulders.

But his sense of relief did not stay with him long. It only lasted until, walking home in the dark a little after the following midnight, he turned the corner within sight of his hotel. The building was lit up like a Christmas tree, and so were the two patrol cars parked in the street in front of it. Jake did not like the look of this. He could only surmise that his actions of the night before had somehow caught up with him, that his pursuers had somehow recognized him and traced him here. But as he stood there wondering what to do now, he saw first one patrol car, then the other, pull out from the curb and drive away. He watched their taillights dwindle out of sight, and then he crossed the street to the hotel entrance.

On any other night he would have found the lobby empty. Tonight he found maybe a dozen people standing together in little groups, talking among themselves. They were a motley crowd in many ways, but they all had the same look of bleary confusion, as if they all had been suddenly roused from sleep. Even the clerk behind the desk seemed to have been shaken out of his usual lethargy. Jake approached him and asked what was going on.

"I guess you missed out on all the fun," he answered. "One of our residents went off his head and started shooting up the place. Walker in 4-D. He came in around eleven and started up to his room same as always. Partway up he went crazy like I said. Pulled out a gun and started shooting. Yelling too, about giant slug monsters trying to get him. Funny thing, when the cops got here he came out to them as quiet as a lamb. It was like he was glad to see them. They packed him into an ambulance and took him over to County General for observation. It's a wonder he didn't kill someone, emptying his gun in the hall like that. And God only knows how he made that stinking mess on the floor."

Jake gave little thought to the clerk's story on the way up to his room. But there was no reason for him to do otherwise. After all, the only part that really concerned him was the fact that the cops had not been here on his account. Anyway, such disturbances were almost inevitable with the sort of clients the hotel catered to. Hardly a week went by without something happening to make life here a little more interesting. As for Jake, the only thing he was interested in now was getting to bed. It had been a long day after a difficult night, and he did not need any obstacles coming between him and sleep.

But the very fact that he did not need obstacles assured that he would get one. He had no sooner set foot on his own floor than he began to notice the smell. The air up here was pretty foul at the best of times, but tonight the usual odors of disinfectant and tobacco smoke were mingled with something new and strange. The new odor was not strange enough to keep Jake from thinking that he had smelled it before. But neither was it familiar enough to help him remember where or when.

A moment later he had tracked it to its source, a wide dark stain running down the center of the carpeted hallway. How had somebody managed to make that? It looked like they had dragged a burlap sack full of waterlogged garbage from one end of the hall to the other. Smelled like it too. The smell had better not have gotten into Jake's room, or there would be hell to pay. The sack must have had some jagged metal in it along with the garbage, because it had left a couple of small but ugly holes in addition to the stain. But they were no ordinary holes, as Jake saw clearly when he looked a little closer. They were bullet holes. And in that same instant he recognized the smell. It was the same heavy animal smell he had encountered last night in the sewer.

He fumbled three times trying to unlock his own door, and when he had it locked behind him he went quickly around the room turning on every light he could find. He was not normally an imaginative man, or one much given to irrational fears. But sometimes you had to be. Sometimes you could not explain things in any other way. A man might go crazy and shoot up a place without having seen anything unusual. And there must be plenty of ways to foul a floor without involving monsters. But when the shooting took place outside your room, when the foulness ended within inches of your door, and when both things came on the same night, the night *after* you brought something up from the sewer, then you would have to be crazy not to see the connection. You would have to be crazy not to see that you had not been alone down there. That whatever had been with you had followed you to the surface. That they wanted the statuette you had stolen and had come to take it back.

He did not know how they had found him. He did not know how they had entered the building unseen. But this much he knew. They had only been checked by their encounter with the shooter. Checked not killed, as the absence of bodies showed. They were gone for now, but they would soon be back. There would not always be a man with a gun to stop them. They would keep coming back again and again until they got what they wanted.

There was only one thing for Jake to do. He would talk to Manny. Manny seemed to know about these things. Manny would be able to tell him what he had to deal with. And if there was no other way, Manny would sell him back the statuette so that he could throw it back to its inhuman worshippers in the depths of their underground world.

But when he arrived at Manny's pawn shop next morning, he found a big white "CLOSED" sign posted in the window. Looking over it though the murky glass, he thought he saw someone moving around in there. He tapped on the glass and rattled the knob to get his attention. He was so intent on what he was doing that he never heard the other man coming up behind him.

"It's closed."

Jake turned on the speaker angrily. "Why don't you—" he began, then stopped when he saw the other, a large man in a brown suit.

"Hello, Lieutenant."

The other was as quick to recognize him. "Jake! Jake Johnson! This *is* a surprise. I haven't seen you since you ratted out your friends over that Exham job, three or four months ago. I hope you're keeping your nose clean."

"Why wouldn't I be, when I know there are smart boys like you waiting to wipe it for me?"

The detective smiled, but not with his eyes. "I'm glad to hear it, Jake. I really am. But you and I both know that Manny Green fronts for one of the biggest fencing operations around. And when I see you loitering outside his door, well, I worry."

"Manny's an old friend. I like to keep in touch with my friends."

"You can't blame me for worrying all the same. An old pro like you doesn't retire, you know. Not in my experience he doesn't. He just goes on until something happens to stop him. Maybe he gets sloppy and careless. Maybe he gets too confident and bites off more than he can chew. Or maybe his luck runs out.

"Like the luck ran out for one of you guys only the other night. Maybe you heard about it on the evening news. He broke into a warehouse a few blocks west of here. One of our officers surprised him and got brained with a crowbar for his trouble. He must have been a real rookie to let the bad guy get behind him like that. But he didn't deserve to have *that* done to him. And the guy who did it shouldn't be allowed to get away with it. Of course he didn't mean to do it. He just panicked in a tight place. He wasn't a killer. He was a professional like you *used* to be, just another regular guy trying to earn a dishonest living. But none of that matters now. What does matter is that the officer died and our boy graduated to the big time."

"That's too bad," Jake said, "for him. But what's it got to do with me?"

"Why, nothing, Jake. Nothing at all. I don't know why I brought it up. Except that a man like you is in a position to hear things, things that could be very useful to us. After all, it wouldn't be the first time you've helped us out, and we've always shown our appreciation. But that's nothing like the appreciation we'd show over this one. A cop-killer is the lowest scum there is, and we're all very anxious to see him brought to justice."

"I'll keep it in mind, Lieutenant."

"You do that, Jake. You do that. Oh, by the way, I hope your business with Manny isn't urgent. It doesn't look like he'll be opening today. As a matter of fact, it looks like he's been shut down for good."

"What do you mean, shut down?"

"We're still trying to figure that out. One of our detectives came out here a couple of hours ago, to try to get a handle on that warehouse job I was telling you about. He found the place still closed, which was odd. But what was even odder was what he saw through the front window. The place looked like a bomb had gone off. Cases smashed, shelves overturned. No sign of Manny anywhere. But the shop was locked up tight the way he would have left it, so maybe he wasn't here when it happened. Maybe."

"Was—was anything taken?"

"That's for somebody else to determine. I don't envy him the job. The mess is bad enough, but with the stink and the slime— What's the matter, Jake? You don't look so good all of a sudden."

"Nothing's the matter. I'm just tired. I didn't get much sleep last night."

"Is that so? You ought to take better care of yourself. Go on home and get some rest. But keep in mind what we talked about. If you *should* hear anything, anything at all, just pick up the phone and give me a call. Or come down to the station and ask for me. You won't be the loser."

After that there was nothing for Jake to do but take the detective's advice and go back to his hotel. But not to sleep. Fear made that impossible.

It was not fear of the cops that kept him awake. Of course the mere fact that the detective had chosen to talk to him about the cop-killing had shaken him at first. But if the detective had had any real reason to connect him to the crime, he would have done more than talk. The cops could not touch him without evidence or witnesses, and they had neither. The only one who could place him at the scene was Jake himself, and he was too smart to give himself away. He had nothing to fear from the cops.

But the slugs were another matter. That was how he had come to think of them: slugs. Walker in 4-D had called them that, and he had actually seen them. Besides, the name was in keeping with the little else Jake knew of them, from the dampness and darkness of their home underground to the sliminess of their trail outside his door. Except that normal slugs were very small, only an inch or two in length. While these, if the width of their trail was any indication, were larger than Jake himself. Normal slugs were purposeless, mindless animals. These were purposeful and cunning.

The pawnbroker could have told him a thing or two about that. Poor Manny! He had not been as fortunate as Jake, to be away when the slugs arrived to reclaim their property. What had they done with him? Maybe they had only killed and eaten him like the animals they were. But they did not behave like animals. It took no more than a strong sense of smell to trace a man or an object through the city streets. But to conceive and worship a god took an intelligence almost human. And to worship a god as hideous as the one the statuette portrayed, the one Manny had called Cthulhu, that took an intelligence evil and perverted, the kind that would delight in having a living victim to punish for daring to possess what was its.

Maybe that was not *all* bad. Now that the slugs had their statuette and Manny, they had no more reason to bother Jake. But that did not mean he was safe. He looked through the window and the fire escape, out over the sleeping city. He had surveyed the same scene any number of times in the last month, without fear. But not tonight. Tonight he could not see the city without thinking of its secret inhabitants, the hidden race of aquatic monsters lurking under it.

Where had they come from? Not from around here, that was for sure. Such things did not belong in the same place as human beings. They must have come from across the sea, from one of the far corners of the world that Manny had talked about. Or they might have come from the sea itself. But wherever they had come from, they were under the city now. *Why* were they here? Had they only settled in the sewers because they found the wet darkness friendly and familiar? Or did they have a more sinister motive? Were they looking for a new source of food? Were they establishing a beachhead, a place from which to stage their raids on the unsuspecting surface dwellers? Were they preparing for nothing less than a full-scale invasion of the land?

Jake did not know. He only knew that he could never feel safe here again. He had to get away, to go someplace farther inland where the slugs could not reach. Maybe he would try Vegas for a while. He had friends there who could put him up for a night or two. He would pack his bag tonight, and then he would try to get a few hours of sleep before morning. And in the morning—

His thoughts were interrupted by a sound, a rhythmic sloshing in the passage outside his room. This was not a good thing for a man in his frame of mind to be hearing. Yet it must have a natural explanation. It must be the cleaning woman scrubbing the carpet in the hallway, scrubbing away the slimy trail outside his door. But why would she be doing that now, when it had already been done that afternoon? And why at one in the morning?

He moved cautiously to the locked door and looked out through the peephole. He saw nothing, nothing but the door across the hall looking swollen and sinister in the distorting lens. But then the view went suddenly black as his own door *thumped* under a heavy blow.

He knew well enough what that blow meant, and he fell back from the door in horror. He had been wrong about the slugs. They were not satisfied with the recovery of their statuette. They were not satisfied with the man in whose possession they had found it. They would only be satisfied with the man who had stolen it from them in the first place. They would only be satisfied with Jake himself.

"Leave me alone!" he screamed at them. "What do you want from me? You got it back, damn you! You got it back!"

But his screams had no effect, unless it was to assure the slugs that they had found him at home. The door bulged slowly inward, the panel splitting from top to bottom with a loud cracking sound. They would be through it in a moment. But when they were they would not find him. He opened the window and climbed out onto the fire escape.

Halfway down he heard the violent crash of the door breaking through. If there were any other sounds, they were lost in the noise of his own rattling descent. And after his feet hit the ground there was only silence. He looked back at the window he had left. The lights had gone out up there, but at least there was no sign of immediate pursuit. But that was no reason to stand here and invite it. He turned and walked quickly toward the lighted street.

And where then? Was the street really so much safer? Maybe for the short term it was. He had relative freedom of movement and a choice of directions for his flight. He was faster than his pursuers, and he could put plenty of distance between himself and them. But what did any of this really buy him? He had had freedom and distance before, when the slugs were in the sewers and he was in his room. If it had not stopped them from finding him then, why should it do so now? Besides, there was only one of him, while there might be tens, even hundreds, of them. More than enough to drive him into a trap, or to close in on him from every side at once.

There was no safety for him in the street. He would have to take cover somewhere. If he could just find a place with lots of people, maybe then he would be safe. But where could he find such a place? This district was all shops and office buildings, all of them closed for the night. Even if there were people inside they would not open to him. Was there no place left for him to hide?

Yes, one place. It was there at the end of the street, its glass doors and windows shining like beacons of hope through the darkness. He ran up the steps and pushed his way in through the double doors. The officer on duty eyed him suspiciously as he approached the desk.

"May I help you?"

"Get me Lieutenant Long."

"Lieutenant Long has gone home for the night. Is there something *I* can help you with?"

Jake hesitated. Then he glanced back over his shoulder to the glass doors and the darkness behind them.

"My name's Johnson, Jake Johnson. I want to turn myself in. I'm the guy who killed the cop in that warehouse job on Monday night."

The confession would be trouble later, but Jake did not care about that. He did not care what they did with him, as long as at the end of it they locked him up in a strong cell where the monsters could not get at him.

He went slowly around the cell, testing its defenses. It was as strong as it could be. The bars that were meant to keep him from getting out would keep anything else from getting in. Besides, nothing could get close enough to try. There was a whole police station in the way, its well-lit corridors full of well-armed men. The slugs could never reach him here. He had beaten them at last.

He stretched himself out on the narrow bed. It was good to be able to relax again. He could not remember the last time he had actually slept. Not since the morning after his adventure in the sewer, nearly two days ago. He had been too afraid, afraid of the cops, afraid of the slugs, to do more than close his eyes in all that time. But there was nothing to be afraid of now. There was nothing to keep him from catching up on his much-needed rest.

What was that? It had sounded like a short burst of bubbles rising through standing liquid. But it had come and gone so quickly that Jake could not be sure. Maybe he had only imagined it. He had spent so much time listening for suspicious noises that it would have been surprising if he had *not* starting supplying them himself. But a good night's sleep would— No, there it was again! And there was no mistaking it this time. Just as there was no mistaking the animal odor that signaled the presence of the slugs.

Jake jumped to his feet. Where could they be coming from? Not from the walls or floor or ceiling. They were too solid to admit anything. Not from the corridor outside his cell. It was too well-lit to let anything approach unseen. That left only the cell itself. Yet how could they have come from here? There was simply no place for anything to hide. The bed was an iron cot with an unobstructed view of the floor beneath. The sink projected from the bare wall. The toilet bowl— Surely they could not have come from that?

He approached the white porcelain bowl and looked down into the clear still water. He had thought himself very clever, getting himself locked up like this. But he was really very stupid. How could he have imagined that there was any place beyond the reach of Cthulhu's vengeful worshippers? The slugs were in the sewers, but the sewers were everywhere. They lay beneath the city in an enormous network, joining every office building, every house, every jail cell. His pursuers had not been frustrated even for a moment by the walls and bars. They had only been waiting for the prisoner to be left alone. And now that he *was* alone—

Suddenly the water began to boil, as if something were pushing its way up through the drain. Jake did not wait to see what would appear. He knew too well already. He turned away from the seething bowl and threw himself against the wall of bars. He pressed his face between the bars and screamed again and again for help.

But even as he did so he wondered why he bothered. He would not be here when help arrived.

# MOTHER OF SERPENTS

The heat of anger that had driven him on his errand had cooled somewhat under the desert stars, so that by the time the cabin was within his reach he could give a thought to caution. He stopped a moment at the edge of the yard, studying the building closely. It seemed a poor thing to be wary of. Its low walls of sun-dried brick were so worn and weathered that they seemed ready to fall back into the clay from which they had been dug. It looked more like a cave than any human habitation. But the light still shone in its vacant doorway, the same red light that had guided him like a sullen beacon through the darkness.

The light had its source in a little fire in a shallow pit in the middle of the floor. But the fire only served to accentuate the cave-like appearance of the room in which it burned. The place was nearly as dark as a cave, for the fire had died down to a few feeble coals. And the air was heavy with bitter smoke, not all of which had managed to escape through the circular hole in the sagging ceiling. But there was little to see here in any case. The single room was bare of furniture, unless that pile of dirty rags in the corner was intended for a bed.

Then the pile of rags moaned and shifted uneasily, like a sleeper troubled by a dream. And looking closer, the young man saw that the pile was not made of rags alone. Slowly, cautiously, he crossed the room to approach the half-seen figure. But he had little reason for such caution. It was only an old woman lying there on a pallet of rags, with a ragged blanket covering her to the chin. It was only a sick old woman. For although it was a temperate night, she seemed to be suffering from extremes of heat and cold. Her body trembled beneath the blanket while her wrinkled face glistened with sweat. Was she asleep or awake? He could not tell. Her eyes were wide and staring, but the balls were blank and dead.

Yet she must have been awake after all, and aware of him in spite of her blindness. For now she turned her face toward his and said in a thin and quavering voice:

"Why are you here, young man?"

And he? What answer could he make to such a question? What words could convey his anger and his pain, and encapsulate the horror of the passing night?

"For Maria," he said softly. "For my wife." And he raised the heavy pistol he carried in his hand.

2

It was an hour after sunset of the same night when the young couple arrived at the inn. Its aspect was not inviting. There were no lights behind the windows, and no voices raised in laughter or song. There were no beasts in the yard beside their own, and the barn was dark and silent. But the travelers were too weary to go elsewhere, even if there had been elsewhere to go.

For a long time there was no answer to their knocking. But then a light came up behind the grate in the door, and a sound of shuffling footsteps. And then the light was blocked by someone's head, and a voice, the voice of a man well on in years, demanded:

"Who is there?"

"We are two travelers," the young man answered, "seeking to avail ourselves of the shelter of your inn."

"Go away!" said the voice. "No honest folk come here at this season, and we do not open our doors to strangers after dark."

"Open the door, old man," said the young one. "We are not robbers, or beggars asking for charity. We can pay for what we need." And he jingled a well-filled purse before him.

The voice did not reply. But presently there came the sound of the bar being lifted, and the door opened inward. The man who opened it was fat and old and slovenly, with a stubble of white beard on his heavy jowls. His nightcap, robe and slippers proclaimed that he had been roused from his bed in spite of the relatively early hour. He admitted the young couple and barred the door behind them.

"I beg your indulgence for the precautions of a nervous old man," he said. "We do not get many travelers so late in the year. And there are robbers hereabout, though few so foolish as to think that there is anything here worth robbing. I see that you have left your beasts in the yard. They shall be tended to, though I must do it all myself. We see too little business nowadays to be able to keep a servant—"

Here he fell silent. He frowned and looked hard at the young man's companion.

"You look troubled, old man," said the young one. "Is something amiss?"

"You did not say that your companion was a woman!"

"And what if she is? She is also my bride, wedded to me in the church at Santa Rosa not three days ago. Now I am taking her from her parents' home to my father's house beyond the mountains. Surely you do not object to a man traveling with his own wife?"

"No, but—"

"Then, since you do not object, perhaps you will show us to our room."

Whatever objection the old man had, he kept it to himself. He led the couple through the common room and along a dark passage. At one point he stopped them before a door. "This is where my wife and I sleep, should you require anything in the night. And this," he said, opening a door a little farther along, "is your room."

The old man led them inside. It was a small room, very plain, with only the one door and a single small window for light and ventilation. A bed, a wardrobe, a washstand and a single chair were all the scanty furniture. The furniture had an air of having seen better days. The brass bedstead was suitably grand, but the mattress was of old sacking stuffed with corn husks.

"You are disappointed with the accommodations," said the old man hopefully. "I cannot blame you. But we are poor folk hereabout, and ill prepared for entertaining people of quality. As the room is not to your liking—"

"The room is very much to our liking," said the young woman, speaking now for the first time. "You are very kind to let us have it."

But the old man, rather than looking pleased at this courtesy, appeared unhappy and subdued. He lowered his eyes to the floor.

"Then I will leave you. Your bed awaits you, as mine does me. May your dreams be nothing but pleasant." And he bowed himself out of the room.

3

The accommodations were poor indeed, but the young people were too weary to find fault with them. Before many minutes had passed they were lying together on the rough mattress, sleeping like children in one another's arms.

But later that night the young man woke to the sound of someone calling his name. It was his wife lying beside him, calling his name in her sleep.

"What is the matter?" he asked her in a low voice. And in a low voice she answered:

"It is the snakes. The room is full of them. They are pouring in through the open window and creeping across the moonlit floor. We cannot escape. They have left us no place to set our feet. Soon they will find the bed."

"You are dreaming," he said. "There are no snakes here. There is nothing to harm you. You are safe in my arms."

His words seemed to quiet her. But he still felt her body trembling against his. Lighting the candle, he found her still asleep, still struggling in the depths of her nightmare. He tried to wake her, but she would not wake, not even when he raised her by the shoulders and shook her. She moaned in protest, and her eyes rolled beneath their delicate lids, but that was all.

The young man was frightened now. He threw on some clothes, hurried out into the passage and pounded on the innkeeper's door. It opened a few inches and the old man peered fearfully out at him through the crack.

*"It is the snakes. The room is full of them. They are pouring in through the open window and creeping across the moonlit floor. We cannot escape. They have left us no place to set our feet. Soon they will find the bed."*

"Is anything wrong, sir?"

"It is my wife. She has fallen into a fever and will not wake. If there is a physician within call, I beg you to send for him at once."

"Alas, sir, there is no physician. The village is too poor to support one. Yet I have heard of a thriving village up the road not half a day's ride from here. If you could take your wife there—"

"My wife is too ill to travel. If there is no physician, then I must care for her myself."

He turned and went back to his own room.

He found his wife no better than when he had left her. There was little enough he could do for her, but what he could he did. He spoke soothing words to calm her restlessness, and bathed her face and arms with cool water to moderate her fever. And after a while his efforts were rewarded by the sight of her puckered brow growing smooth again, her breathing becoming slow and regular. But a short time later her restlessness returned.

"What troubles you, little one?" he asked her in a low voice. "Is it the snakes again?" And in a low voice she answered:

"No. The smaller snakes have joined together to form a single great one. How horrible it is! Its body is as thick as the neck of a horse. It fills the room with its coils. I fear it will loop them over me and crush me like a bird."

"Do not fear," said her husband. "It is only a dream, and a dream can never harm you. I will stay beside you through the night, and you will dream of happier things."

Presently a timid knock came at the door. The young man went and opened it to discover the ample figure of his host and another standing a little behind him. This other was so like the old man in figure and dress that only the relative smoothness of the chin served to show that it was a woman.

"Please pardon this intrusion," the old man said in a low voice. "My wife and I have come to inquire after the health of your poor young lady. Is she any better?"

"You may see for yourself," said the young one bitterly, and stepped aside to let the other pass. But although the other looked into the room where the sick woman lay, he did not cross the threshold. Instead he turned back to her husband.

"Oh, sir, again I ask you to take the young lady away from here. This is not a healthy place for a beautiful young woman. It is particularly bad now, when the season of autumn is upon us. You have already seen how your poor wife suffers under its influence. If you take her away there is still a hope that she may recover. But if you keep her here—" He spoke no more, but dropped his hands to his sides in an eloquent gesture of finality.

The young man was unmoved by this petition. "I thank you for your concern. But I do not believe that one place or one season is more or less healthy than another. I will not endanger my wife's health by subjecting her to the rigors of the road while her fever is upon her. We will stay. If you cannot help me to care for her, then you must leave me to do it alone." And he closed the door in the old people's faces.

These words had been spoken at the door in little more than whispers, yet seemingly they had been loud enough to disturb the patient within. For on returning to the sickbed the young man was delighted to find his wife awake.

"Where are you, Alonso?"

"I am here, little one. I am beside you holding your hand."

"Stay close to me, Alonso. I am afraid. I feel so weak, and my sleep is troubled with nightmares."

"Do not distress yourself, my heart. You are sick with a fever, but it will not last forever. Rest and sleep. Tomorrow you will be well again. Then we will continue our journey beyond the mountains to my father's house, where we will dwell in happiness to the end of our days."

"There was someone at the door."

"It was no one. Only the master and mistress of the house. They want me to take you away from here. They think that the air is bad for you, and that you cannot get well until we leave. They are very foolish."

"Then I am foolish too, for I believe as they do. I feel that an evil cloud surrounds me here, and that if I do not leave quickly I shall die. Take me away, Alonso. My husband, take me away."

"Hush, hush, little one. You frighten yourself with shadows. Besides, you are too ill to travel. You must not let the superstitious beliefs of ignorant peasants rob you of your needed rest."

"But I dream, Alonso! Such dreadful dreams! I dreamed that the room was full of snakes, snakes hiding under the bed and in the drawers of the press and coiled in the washing bowl. Only it was not many snakes at all, but the coils of one great serpent that filled the corners of the room. One great serpent that caught me in its coils and crushed me so that I could not breathe."

"It was only a dream, Maria. And in any case there are no snakes here now. Look!" And he held the candle high so that its light filled the whole room, to show her that they were alone. But the action did not calm her as he had hoped. For suddenly her grip tightened on his arm, and her eyes stared past him toward the open window.

"Who is there?" she cried.

"There is no one. Who do you think is there?"

"It is the woman, the old woman of my dreams. The horrible old woman with the body of a serpent, who laughs in my face while she crushes out my life. Oh, do not let her come near me, Alonso! Do not let her come near me!"

"But Maria, there is no one there!" And indeed there was not, not even so much as a shadow cast by the light of the flickering candle.

"There is! She is coming toward me, rolling her blind eyes and grinning with her toothless mouth. And all the while she speaks to me of the horrors that are in store for me. She reaches for me with her skinny hand. Do not let her touch me, Alonso! If she touches me I shall die! Mother of God! She is—"

These words were the last she ever spoke. For then she screamed and fell back upon the mattress from which she had partly risen. And when her husband caught her to his breast he felt her dead in his arms.

## 4

After a while the young man returned to the bedroom of the innkeeper and his wife. They looked like a pair of owls, sitting upright in bed with their blankets pulled under their chins and their eyes big and round, sitting as they must have sat since hearing the young woman's dying scream. The young man entered without knocking and stood quietly at the foot of the bed. His bowed head made it difficult to read the expression on his face. But there was no mistaking the heavy pistol he carried at his side.

It was the innkeeper's wife who broke the silence.

"This is a terrible thing that has happened, sir, a terrible thing. But you must not think that my husband and I are to blame. We were wrong to admit you, I know. But you were so insistent, and we are so very poor, and your gold was a great temptation for us. And we honestly thought that the old woman was dead.

"We were mad to think it. We see that now. It is more than half a century since last she visited us, or a light has been seen burning in her doorway. But what is half a century to one who is high in the favor of the Evil One? And such is the old woman whom we call the Mother of Serpents.

"My husband told you that this is an unhealthy place. It is also an accursed place, for the power of Hell is strong here. Here Satan and his attendant devils hold court in the desert by night in the form of giant snakes. And here the heathen red men used to meet to worship him with blasphemous rites under the name of Yig, the Father of Serpents. The red men are all gone now, driven from the land with fire and sword by the valiant soldiers of Christ. But the Mother of Serpents remains.

"The Mother of Serpents is the priestess of Yig. She lives alone in her little hut in the desert north of the village. No one knows how long she has been there. She was certainly there before the Christians came, and some believe that she was there before the heathens as well. Either way, she must be very old. She must have died long years ago, were it not in her power to extend her life with the lives of the young women she visits in their dreams.

"It is always young women she preys upon, as if they alone can provide her with the kind of life she requires. It is always the same. On a night of the autumn season a young woman falls ill with a fever. It is not a natural fever, because it is accompanied by unnatural dreams. Always they are the same dreams, of serpents, and of the old woman who is the Mother of Serpents. And always, always the fever ends in the young woman's death.

"It does not happen often, maybe twice in a hundred years. But that is because the people here know how to protect themselves. Parents with daughters of marriageable age find husbands for them far from here. Or they send them away for the autumn months or take them to new homes elsewhere. The region is nearly deserted now. Yet it is many years since the last time it happened. I was but a small girl then, and I am nearly sixty now. Is it any wonder we began to hope that the Mother of Serpents was dead at last?

"That is why we let you stay, in spite of the season, in spite of your wife's beauty and youth. But when you told my husband that your wife had fallen ill, we knew that it had started all over again. My husband begged you to take her away. He did not tell you about the Mother of Serpents, because he knew that you would laugh at him. But he begged you nonetheless. We did what we could, young sir. Do us the justice to remember that. And do not, I pray, revenge your so great loss on us."

The young man's face hardened as he listened to this speech. He believed the old couple now, though it had taken the death of his young wife to convince him. But if his belief had not come in time to show him how to save her life, at least it had shown him how to avenge her death.

Something of this must have been reflected in the young man's eyes. "Oh, sir," cried the horrified innkeeper's wife, "you must not think that the Mother of Serpents is subject to human vengeance. Many have thought that in the past, and have gone into the desert in search of her. They were all young and strong as you are, but none has ever returned. Her children the serpents protect her. And where their protection will sometimes fail, the protection of Yig will not. So accept your wife's death with piety and patience, or you will cast away your own life after hers."

But these last words were spoken in vain. The young man had already left the room.

5

"For Maria," said the young man quietly. "For my wife." And he aimed his pistol at the sick old woman's heart.

The woman could not see his pistol, but she must have recognized the threat in his voice. Yet her own voice was calm and steady as she said:

"Your wife is with me. Here, I will show her to you."

Of course he knew that she was lying. So it must have been the enormity of her lie that made him hold his fire, that made him lower his useless weapon while the old woman rose to her feet. The ragged blanket slipped down from her shoulders to fall in a heap about her ankles, leaving her body naked. Her wrinkled hide hung upon her like an ill-fitting garment. Her breasts and belly sagged before her like wineskins three-quarters empty. The young man frowned in disgust. But her blind eyes could not see his expression, or else it only amused her. She opened her toothless mouth to laugh at him.

Or was it to laugh at him? Certainly no sound came forth. There was something in her mouth that must have stopped the passage of any sound, something black and shiny that bulged from between her distended jaws. She raised her clawed hands to her lips and hooked them into the elastic skin. And as the young man watched in speechless horror, she stretched and tore the wrinkled skin back and down in hideous folds, uncovering an object as large and round as a human head, as black and shiny as a human face behind a curtain of thick black hair.

The hands continued to claw the wrinkled hide, dragging it lower and lower. Now a pair of smooth white shoulders emerged where the blotched old ones had been. Now the empty wineskin breasts gave place to two full round ones. And so it went, curve by curve, limb by limb, until there stood before him not a horrible old woman, but a slender and beautiful young one, stepping from the witch's castoff skin as from a discarded petticoat. And when the small hands rose to part the heavy hair and reveal the face behind it, it was the face of his own dear wife he saw, smiling at him with her warm brown eyes, her full red lips and small white teeth.

What miracle was this that had brought his Maria back to him? He did not know, but neither did he question it. It was enough to know that she was here before him now, smiling at him her welcoming smile, gliding toward him with her arms extended to enfold him in a lover's embrace. And then her slender body was pressed against him, her arms twined around him like serpents. How strong she was! Her embrace was painfully tight. He would have protested, but he could not draw sufficient breath to do so.

All this while she had been silent. She had only smiled that loving smile which had no need of words. But now her red lips parted as if she would speak to him. Her small mouth opened in a tremendous yawn, a yawn almost beyond the power of human jaws to encompass. Even so had the old woman yawned in giving birth to the young one. But maybe the pain and want of air were causing him to imagine things. Certainly there was nothing black and shiny in this woman's mouth. There was only a hungry darkness waiting to be filled.

# FAST FOOD

On the day that Belial's Burgers opened its doors for the first time, Dennis came down with Carl and Ron to help celebrate the occasion. A restaurant opening was always an occasion, especially if the restaurant was close by and relatively inexpensive. Belial's could hardly be closer, standing as it did across the street from their downtown office building. And the food could not be cheaper, not while it was being given away as part of an opening-day promotion.

The prospect of a free lunch had brought out more than Dennis and his friends. The restaurant was so crowded that it took them a good ten minutes to get to the counter and place their orders, and another five to get a table where they could sit and wait for their food. But even with the crowding and the attendant delays, the three were impressed with what they saw. The dining room was clean, bright and pleasant. The tables and chairs were sufficiently comfortable, and positioned at an adequate distance from the tables and chairs around them. Most new restaurants took a couple of months to hit their stride, but not this one. The workers moved through it with drilled efficiency, with almost military precision.

The military impression was partly created by the uniformity of the workers themselves. This was more than the sameness of their white tee shirts and black pants, their white cloth aprons and paper caps. There was a sameness of figure and face as well, a roundness of form and a darkness of complexion that suggested at least an ethnic tie if not a family one. Also they were uniformly plump and sleek.

"But that's a good thing," Carl pointed out. "How tasty could the food be if even the help wouldn't eat it?"

The workers' efficiency was more than show, for its effects were visible everywhere. Even at the table where the three friends sat. They were not the first or even the second party to sit there, yet they could not tell from its appearance. It was spotlessly clean and mirror-bright, and neatly laid out with napkin dispenser, with ketchup and mustard bottles, with all the little touches that one looks for in such a place but does not always find.

There was even a little dish of advertising matchbooks. These last were so unusual in appearance that Dennis had to pick one up for a closer look. Its most prominent feature was Belial's striking logo, a field of fiery red stamped with a design in deepest black, the stylized silhouette of a burger upraised on a three-tined pitchfork. But the logo was surrounded with an intricate inscription, in letters and words so weirdly exotic that Dennis could not even be sure they were English.

"Yog-Sothoth," he read aloud.

"How's that again?" Carl asked.

"It's printed on the cover. 'Yog-Sothoth is the Gate.' But what's Yog-Sothoth?"

"Maybe a food additive," Ron suggested.

Then the food arrived, on three trays brought by two smiling workers who left as quickly as they came. The true measure of any burger joint is of course its burgers, and whoever had assembled these was a master of the art. Everything about them was beautiful, from the billowing crowns of the seeded buns, through the colorful layers of ripe red tomato, crisp green lettuce, white onion and yellow cheese, to the generous patties of fresh ground beef charbroiled to perfection. Dennis took his in both hands and raised it to his watering mouth in eager anticipation. Then he stopped and wrinkled his nose.

"Something wrong, Dennis?" Carl asked through his own first mouthful.

"It smells funny. I think the meat's gone bad."

"Really? Mine's okay. What about yours, Ron?"

Ron nodded, his mouth too full to speak.

"Well, mine's not," Dennis insisted. "It stinks to high heaven. Here, smell for yourself."

He reached it across the table toward Carl, who leaned over to take a cautious sniff.

"Smells fine to me. Are you sure it's the burger?"

Dennis pulled it back again. Could he have been mistaken? He raised it to his own nose and felt his gorge rise in response. He threw it back on the tray.

"I can't eat this. It makes me sick just thinking about it. Excuse me. I've got to get some air."

And he practically ran for the exit.

The burger episode, as it came to be called, had no effect on Belial's subsequent business. The restaurant's success over the next two weeks was nothing short of miraculous. The opening had already drawn about a quarter of the people in Dennis's building. And with those who had gone talking up the place to those who had not, it was not long before the other three quarters had joined them. But the real secret of Belial's success was that no one who had eaten there ever wanted to eat anywhere else. Some even went there two or three times a day.

The only one who stayed away was Dennis himself. His friends had forgotten the episode almost at once. At least, they had stopped teasing him about it after the first or second day. But he could not put it behind him so easily. There was no good reason for this, as he would have been the first to admit. He had gotten a bad burger. So what? That could happen anywhere.

Besides, it was not as if he had eaten it or been hurt by it in any way. He was not even out the price of a meal. Nevertheless the experience had left a bad taste in his mouth. He was not inclined to repeat it.

But why should he repeat it? No one was forcing him to eat there. There were plenty of other fast food places within easy reach of the office. He could eat at a different one every day of the week without even considering Belial's. The only problem, if you could call it a problem, was that he could only do it alone. Everyone else was at Belial's.

"How can you keep going back to that place?" he asked Carl one day after turning down his invitation to lunch there for the sixth or seventh time. "I'd be bored out of my skull by now."

"I don't know," Carl answered. "If it was any other place, maybe I would be too. Maybe I will be soon enough. But until then, why kick? The place is right across the street, so it couldn't be more convenient. The prices are reasonable. And the food, the food is. . . ."

He seemed at a loss to say what the food was. But his face beamed at the memory.

"Oh, come on," Dennis said. "It can't be as good as all that. When you get right down to it, the best burger in the world is still just bread and meat."

Carl shook his head, saddened by his friend's unwillingness to understand.

"Maybe. And maybe you wouldn't say that if you tried one. Sure you won't join us?"

"I can't. I have that report to get out."

"Some other time. Now I'd better get down there. The place fills up pretty fast these days."

Dennis had not been entirely honest with Carl. He had no report to get out, at least none that could not wait till after lunch. But he was less embarrassed to lie to his friend than to let him know the truth. It was not that Dennis did not *want* to join the others. His inability to share in their pleasures made him feel awkward and lonely, as if everyone else had gone to a party and only he was left behind. But he could not think about the place without remembering that atrocious burger smell. He could not think of eating there without his stomach turning over in protest.

Dennis did not have much leisure to think about Belial's in the days and weeks that followed. As the restaurant's star continued its rise, his company's star began a steep decline. It was hard to say what was behind this. Probably it was no one thing, but several things in combination. Tardiness was up. Absenteeism too. A kind of malaise infected the work force. The employees who still came in might have been enough to hold the place together, but they seemed uninterested in the task. The entire workload had to be shouldered by the few employees, Dennis included, who still did any work.

But Belial's would not allow itself to be ignored forever. Returning from the washroom late one morning about a month after the restaurant's opening, Dennis was surprised to see one of the restaurant's workers coming out of his and Carl's office. The worker smiled and nodded as they passed. It was probably meant to be friendly, but to Dennis it seemed a little sinister, as if the man knew something to his disadvantage.

Carl was eating a burger at his desk when Dennis came in and told him what he had seen.

"Yes," Carl said between bites, "they deliver now. It'll be a big help now that we're stuck here in the office all day. I don't know why they didn't think of it before. Oh, I got something for you, too."

He pushed a white paper bag across the desk toward Dennis. Dennis felt a sudden twinge of nausea. But it passed when he turned his eyes away.

"Too bad," he said then. "I was hoping they had sent us a temp. I don't see any other way out of this mess. What's wrong with this place, Carl?"

"That's a tall order. Where do you want me to start?"

"What's wrong with the people? Hardly anyone comes to work anymore. Nearly a third of the staff was out yesterday, and it's worse today. And it's the same in the other departments."

"People get sick, you know."

"Yes, but the ones who *do* come in are just as bad. They spend half the day asleep at their stations, and the other half wandering around in a daze. The only time they show any life is at lunchtime. Look at Wendy, the department secretary. I can't remember when she wasn't on a diet. She isn't on one now, though. Now she eats like she's trying to make up for all those missed meals."

"Well, *I* think it's an improvement. Wendy was always too skinny for my taste. She looks better now than she has in years."

"But it's not just Wendy. It's Ron, too, before he dropped out of sight. It's—"

Dennis stopped, suddenly aware that he was talking about Carl as well. The last few weeks had changed his friend greatly. The change had been gradual, so gradual that Dennis had failed to notice it. Yet how could he *not* have noticed it? Carl must have packed another fifty pounds on his already ample frame. He had been large before, but now he loomed over his desk like a prize hog masquerading as a man. Dennis felt sick all over again. But if Carl suspected the cause of his silence, he did not show it.

"They're probably just tired and bored," he said as he finished off the last remnants of his burger. "Of course they are. After all the hours we've been putting in, we could do with a nap ourselves. No wonder you're feeling crabby. But you'll feel better when you've had your lunch."

Dennis did not look at the bag again. "I—I just had something out of the machine."

"Well, it won't be much good cold. Since *you* don't want it, do you mind if I—"

Dennis did not answer. He fled back to his own desk and buried himself in his work, distancing himself as far as possible from the other's display of hoggish enjoyment.

That night Dennis had to work even later than usual. It was nearly eleven when he clocked out and went down to the bus stop in front of the building. At this time of night the street was dark and dead. The brightest place on it was Belial's storefront directly across from him, and its light was mostly confined to the red and black logo of the burger and pitchfork above its window. Most stores left their blinds open at night, on the theory that a thief would not break into a place whose interior was clearly visible. Belial's blinds were closed.

But even at this late hour the street was not *completely* dead. A lone pedestrian was coming toward him along the opposite side. Dennis watched the man with casual interest, grateful to have something besides Belial's to occupy his attention. But as the man drew nearer his interest turned to fascination. The pedestrian was such a strange figure to see out in public. He was enormously fat. He moved slowly and rather stiffly, as Dennis imagined a sleepwalker might move. But the strangest thing about him was his clothes. He was wearing a tent-like overcoat over what appeared to be pajamas and slippers.

But the surprise Dennis felt at seeing this figure was nothing compared to the surprise he felt a moment later when the figure came even with Belial's. Because there it fell in with several other figures standing like sleeping cattle just outside the restaurant door. These new figures must have been standing around the corner earlier. At least, Dennis could think of no better explanation for their sudden appearance now. There were about a dozen of them, men and women in assorted colors, shapes and sizes. But all of them were grotesquely fat, all of them squeezed into incongruous outfits several sizes too small for them.

Who were these people? What were they doing here? Were they a secret club of burger addicts trying to score a last fix before bedtime? Maybe that was not so far from the truth. Because a moment later the restaurant door opened, spilling a flood of light out onto the silent crowd, which proceeded to file through it one by one like a parade of circus elephants. And it was then that Dennis got the biggest surprise of all. As each figure approached the doorway its face was clearly lit, and the third from the end was a face that he recognized. It was Carl.

Dennis could not believe his eyes. Carl here? But he had left the office hours ago. Why had he come back now? Dennis was so dumbfounded that for a moment it did not occur to him to cross the street and ask. And by the time it *did* occur to him, it was already too late. The last figure had disappeared inside. A restaurant worker, easily recognizable by his white cap and apron, appeared in the doorway, apparently on the lookout for stragglers. His eyes fastened on Dennis for an uncomfortably long time. Then he withdrew and closed the door.

Carl was not at the office when Dennis arrived next morning. That was nothing unusual these days when almost everyone came in late who bothered to come in at all. But it was harder than usual on Dennis, because he wanted to talk to Carl about what he had seen last night in front of the restaurant. He waited for him for two full hours. Then he called down to the front desk to ask if anyone there had heard from him. The receptionist, a harried temp, said that Carl had not called in sick. Nobody ever called in sick. They just stopped coming in.

A little alarm went off inside Dennis's head, but he was still not ready to give up. He remembered that he had Carl's home number in his address file. He found it and called it.

"Hello," said a familiar voice at the other end.

"Hello, Carl. It's—"

But the voice had not stopped talking.

". . . can't come to the phone right now. But leave your name and number and I'll get back to you when I can."

Dennis left a message asking Carl to call him. After that there was nothing to do but sit and wait for Carl to get back to him. But he was finding it very hard to sit and wait. The little alarm inside his head was louder now, and increasingly difficult to ignore. He was no longer only frustrated by his inability to question his friend. He was also afraid. Afraid that Carl had dropped out of sight like all the rest. Afraid that Belial's Burgers was behind it.

He went to the window and looked out and down at the restaurant three stories below him. It looked small and unimportant down there, closed in on two sides by tall office buildings and by a windowless warehouse behind. Who would believe that such an insignificant-looking place could have done away with all those people? But he could no longer ignore the facts. The fact that those who ate there lost all desire to eat anywhere else. The fact that they went on eating there until they grew fat in body and dull in mind. The fact that they kept growing fatter and duller until they returned to the restaurant late one night and were never seen or heard from again. All these facts added up to one inescapable conclusion: The restaurant was putting something in its food, something to turn its patrons into dependent, obedient slaves.

No wonder Dennis had reacted to his burger so strongly. The wonder was that he had been the only one to react. Why? He did not know the answer to that question. But he was grateful for it, whatever it was. Without it, he would have ended up a fat, mindless zombie like the others. Why was the restaurant doing this? He did not know the answer to that question, either. Maybe it was a front for an international slave ring. Or maybe it was a cult. But it did not really matter *why* the restaurant was doing what it did. What mattered was making it stop.

He went from the window back to his desk, picked up the phone and started to call the police. But halfway through the number he paused. It was one thing to know the truth, another to convince others of it. What was he going to say to them? People were eating at a fast food place? Since when was that evidence of a crime? They were not coming to work or answering their phones? How could he go to the police with that? They would laugh at him or, worse, lock him up as a dangerous lunatic. It was no use calling them now. He would have to wait until tomorrow when he had something more definite to tell them.

As he hung up the phone he noticed something on his desktop, a little square of red and black cardboard half buried among his usual papers. He picked it up and examined it, though he already knew what it was. There was no mistaking the familiar form of an advertising matchbook. There was no mistaking Belial's familiar burger and pitchfork logo. What was the thing doing there? Maybe Carl had dropped it. Maybe the cleaning crew had found it on the floor and returned it to the wrong desk. But however it had gotten there, it was going away now. He started to crumple it up and toss it in the wastebasket, then changed his mind and pocketed it instead.

That day Dennis finished his work early, for the simple reason that there was no one left to assign him any more. But he hung around the office till long after closing time anyway. At half past ten he clocked out and went down to his usual bus stop. But he had no intention of catching the bus. His only purpose was to keep an eye on Belial's.

He waited about a quarter of an hour before anything happened. Then, just as on the previous night, the patrons came to line up at Belial's door. Just as on the previous night, the door opened to admit them. Just as on the previous night, a lone worker came out to look for stragglers, then followed the others inside.

Dennis waited a few minutes longer. Then he walked across the empty street to Belial's front window. The blind was closed, but there enough space between it and the window frame to allow him at least a partial view of the dining room and the people inside it. The people were standing in a long line across the front of the counter, side by side, facing outward, with a number of restaurant workers walking up and down in front of them. They looked like a group of military officers reviewing a line of fat, dejected troops.

Dennis watched the proceedings in puzzled fascination. Without a doubt there was something going on here, something more than a bunch of burger fanatics lining up for a midnight snack. But what? He would have to wait for them to show him. But evidently they were not going to show him. All at once, as if in response to a spoken command, the fat people turned and started filing around the counter to disappear through a door behind it. All at once the dining room was empty except for two workers who had stayed behind in quiet conversation. And a moment later these also turned and followed the others out.

But Dennis could not let his investigation end there. It was far too important for that. If he could not move it forward by looking through the window, then he would have to do so by going through the door. It would be dangerous, but maybe less dangerous than it seemed. The workers would not be expecting him, and they would be too preoccupied with their invited guests to notice an uninvited one.

But he would have to catch them first. That might not be so easy. He was already behind them when he began, and he could not close the distance without putting himself at more risk than he could bear. The unlocked door presented no obstacle, and the clean, bright dining room behind it was as empty as it had appeared from the outside. But the door behind the counter was trickier, even with a little round window in its midst surveying the room behind it. This was a kitchen even cleaner and brighter than the dining room, and no less empty of human beings.

At the back of the kitchen was another door. In any normal establishment it would have opened onto an alley or a parking lot. Here it opened onto a long, narrow corridor with several more doors on either side. The corridor was empty for most of its length, but about halfway down a collection of cardboard boxes was lined up under one wall. Dennis supposed that these open boxes contained restaurant supplies of various sorts, as indeed their markings indicated. But as he got closer he saw that their markings had nothing to do with their contents. The boxes were full of articles of clothing wadded carelessly together. And it did not take him long to recognize some of these articles as having been worn by the fat people who came this way before him. But if the garments he recognized had been worn by the fat people, what of those he did not? It was too much to suppose that the people had *all* stopped here to shed their clothes into these boxes before going on again, a line of naked human blobs like fattened cattle driven to the slaughter.

Cattle driven to the slaughter! The thought stunned Dennis like a sledgehammer blow. What kind of men could sink so low? And yet, what other explanation could fit the facts so well? He had assumed that the restaurant was turning its patrons into slaves. But the restaurant did not want slaves. It wanted meat. It did not support itself by the labor of slaves. It did so

*But when he turned back the way he came, he found that it was already too late. A couple of restaurant workers had entered the corridor behind him. They were standing shoulder to shoulder between him and the way out, smiling and brandishing what appeared to be lengths of sawed-off broomstick.*

by murdering its old patrons and feeding them to new ones. The boxes of clothing were the proof. And even if they were not, it no longer mattered to Dennis. He had his own flesh and blood to look out for. If even half of what he believed about the restaurant was true, it would not hesitate to murder him to keep its activities from becoming known. And if the other half was true as well, it would not have any trouble disposing of the evidence. He had to get out now.

But when he turned back the way he came, he found that it was already too late. A couple of restaurant workers had entered the corridor behind him. They were standing shoulder to shoulder between him and the way out, smiling and brandishing what appeared to be lengths of sawed-off broomstick. No wonder Dennis had been able to get so deep into the restaurant without any check or hindrance. The restaurant had been drawing him into a trap. And now the trap was sprung. The workers stopped smiling and started walking purposefully toward him. But Dennis did not wait to meet them. He turned and ran.

The corridor went straight for ten more yards and then turned sharply to the left. The new stretch was nearly as long as the old one, but there was only one door in all its length, a door opening on the right side about halfway down. It had a placard tacked to it, a little cardboard rectangle with the words "To the Gate" neatly hand-lettered on its clean white face. Dennis did not know what gate that was, but it sounded enough like a way out to be promising. He tried the knob and found it unlocked. He took a last look back down the hall. His pursuers were still invisible, but the sound of their running footsteps showed that they would not be so much longer. He slipped through the door and closed it softly behind him.

No sooner had he closed it than he wished it open again. The darkness was so complete that for a moment he thought he had been struck blind. He felt along the door for the knob, thinking to open it just long enough to get his bearings. But his exploring hand found no knob, only a cold metal plate where a knob should have been. The door could not be opened from this side at all. But that was not necessarily a bad thing. To open it now would almost certainly give him away to his pursuers. Still, his inability to do so significantly narrowed his options. He had nowhere to go but forward.

He set out slowly, groping his way with outthrust hands. Damn this darkness anyway! His eyes should be used to it by now, yet his blindness was as total as at the moment he had shut himself in. But the darkness was not the only thing he had to contend with. There was also the smell. A faint, unpleasant odor of sickrooms and slaughterhouses, of open sewers and open graves. An odor he had learned long ago to associate with Belial's. Maybe it was reasonable for the place to smell like Belial's. But that did not make

Dennis any more comfortable, or any less desperate to find the way out. If only he had some means of making a light, a flashlight or—

He cursed himself for the idiot he was. Because he *did* have the means. He had the book of matches, the one he had found on his office desktop. He took it from his pocket and opened it, tore out a match and struck it on the igniting strip. The match flared up brightly, blinding him all over again. But almost at once it settled down to a steady point of warm yellow flame. He raised it over his head and looked around. But there was nothing to see, nothing but the concrete floor beneath his feet stretching flat and empty as far as his little light could reach. What was this place? It was too large to be contained in the restaurant building itself. It might be—it surely was—the warehouse *behind* the restaurant, the one that stretched between it and the next street. Which meant that the gate must be somewhere ahead.

Then the first match burned out, and he threw it away and struck a second one. And then he saw that he was no longer alone. The people were in there with him. They were standing quiet and motionless in a little crowd about a dozen feet in front of him. Of course they were the same people. There could not be another gathering of people so grotesquely naked, so hideously obese. Only now they did not seem so sluggish. They looked like a strange and repellent dance troop frozen in mid-dance. Their limbs were twisted in rigid agony, their jaws stretched wide in silent screams. But the strangest thing about them was their feet. Several of them were hanging as much as a yard above the floor, and none of them approached it any closer than six inches.

This last was so improbable that Dennis felt sure he had made a mistake. But before he could discover the cause of his error, the second match burned down to his fingers and he shook it out reflexively. And when he had struck a third, he found that he had something much larger to deal with. The dancers had not changed their positions at all, yet the whole troop had managed to glide about six feet closer to him. And it was gliding closer still.

Dennis did not wait to see any more. He turned and ran. His match went out in the wind of his flight, but he did not stop to light another. He could not bear the thought of that mad troop catching up to him, not now when he knew what it meant. He had only been half right before. The restaurant was fattening its patrons for food, that much was true. But it was not feeding them to other patrons, nor was it eating them itself. Dennis saw everything clearly now, because he had seen that the naked figures were not just hanging in the air. They were embedded like so much fruit cocktail in the belly of some invisible gelatin beast.

That beast was close behind him now. He could locate it by the sound it made, a wobble of displaced air like a sheet of tin being shaken to simulate thunder. But he still had one thing in his favor. The beast was used to its meals being mindless and slow. It had never had to deal with *fast* food before.

Fast food! His brain laughed even as it screamed. Fast food! He only hoped that the food was fast enough to—

# UNDERSTUDY

It started with the monster. Before it ended, an actress was frightened into hysterics on a working set in broad daylight, and two men disappeared from a seaside bungalow in the middle of the night. The police who investigated it were too inclined to dismiss it. They thought the studio had rigged it as a publicity stunt for the new picture. But I know better. I was there. I watched it happen from the first.

I had considerable experience with monsters in those days, working in the Galactic Pictures makeup department at the height of the fifties science fiction boom. But the Fish Man was going to be something special. I don't mean the creature itself. That was just another bug-eyed horror, just another missing link between sea life and land life, such as must have been featured in maybe a dozen pictures before and since. No, what would make the Fish Man special was the makeup. For one thing, it had to be a full-figure suit, and that had never been done before. For another, it had to be suitable for swimming in.

But these problems were relatively easy to solve, given time and money and a staff of talented people. The real trick was to make the monster conform to the ideas of the producers. They knew what they wanted, I guess, but they couldn't communicate their desires in any meaningful way. They could only tell us when we had failed to meet them. It wouldn't have been so bad if they had always recognized our failures in the design stages. But sometimes it took a finished suit to show them exactly where we had gone wrong. Then there was nothing to do but stand looking on while several weeks' work got carted away with the rest of the garbage.

I was complaining about this to Ted Marsh that Saturday afternoon on the porch of his Venice bungalow. Ted was my best friend in the department, and he used to have me over to drink beer and watch the pelicans fish in the surf. But today I wasn't much interested in pelicans. Today I only wanted to let off steam over this latest in a long series of workplace disasters. And Ted, always the perfect host, sat quietly by and let me do it. He sat quietly by, that is, until somewhere around the middle of my fourth beer.

"Maybe it wasn't *all* the producers' fault," he said then. "That last design wasn't exactly wonderful."

"Wasn't exactly wonderful! You've got *that* right. With those lobster claws and that lizard tail, it looked more like a bad case of the DT's than a product of earthly evolution. Lobster claws! My five-year-old nephew could do better than that. We could do better ourselves, if we were a little more sober."

"We could—" Ted began, then lapsed into silence. For a long time he sat like that, saying never a word, just staring out over the ocean as if he had forgotten that I was there.

This sort of thing was not unusual. Ted was an odd fish at the best of times. Oh, he was nice enough when you got to know him, but more than a little eccentric. But maybe his odd behavior went with his odd appearance. Ted was nobody's idea of handsome. With his pop eyes and flat nose, his wide mouth and receding chin, he looked more like a frog than a man.

As I said, this sort of thing was not unusual. I guessed that he was tired of the subject, so I turned the talk to other things. But on Monday he came to work a good fifteen minutes late, with a great big artist's portfolio under his arm.

"What have you got there?" I asked him.

"I'll tell you that later."

Then, as the Old Man passed through the shop on his way to his office at the back, Ted gathered up his portfolio.

"Wish me luck," he said.

"What for?"

"I'll tell you that later, too."

Before I could answer, he turned away and started toward the Old Man's door. He knocked and went inside and didn't come out again for a long time. When the door did open maybe half an hour later, it was the Old Man himself who came out to call the rest of us in to a departmental meeting. I went in with everyone else, and saw Ted standing at the back of the room looking nervous and excited. But I forgot all about him when I saw his big portfolio lying open on the table.

Nowadays the Fish Man has become so familiar that it's hard to appreciate the striking originality of the design. Well, it was the original design I was seeing now. It was all there. The body armored in overlapping plates of horny reptilian hide. The oversized hands and feet, with webbing between the whole lengths of the fingers and toes, and wicked-looking claws at the tips. The weird head, noseless and chinless, with bulging eyes, a thick-lipped gash of a mouth, and instead of ears, a fringe of gills growing down around the curves of the jaws. It was a monster, all right, and ugly enough to satisfy even the most demanding producer. But it made me smile all the same. For clearly Ted had put a lot of himself into it. Except for the webs and gills and things, it looked like an extreme caricature of his own peculiar physiognomy.

After the meeting I cornered him at his work bench. "So that was your big secret, you mysterious bastard," I said jokingly. "I didn't know you had it in you. Where did you get the imagination to dream up something like that?"

"What imagination?" he answered, his face a perfect deadpan. "I drew it from life."

After that we had our work cut out for us. For the next several weeks we labored to translate Ted's design into three dimensions. We sculpted and cast, painted and tested, then sculpted all over again. In many ways this was a reprise of the work we had been doing for the last three months or more. But there was one thing that made it different, and that was our belief in the new design. There wasn't one of us who didn't think that we were working on something big this time. There wasn't one of us who didn't think that this new creature, from the warts of its domed head to the claws of its great webbed feet, had the potential to take on a life of its own. And the first time the Old Man led Frank Sellers out on the floor in full Fish Man regalia and announced, "Well, boys and girls, it looks like we've got our monster," there wasn't one of us who was inclined to disagree.

Frank was the man in the monster suit. He had been involved in the project from the very beginning, since the suit was built over casts of his body to ensure that it would fit him like a second skin. This made it a large skin to fill. Frank was an athlete, a professional dancer and a strong swimmer, important assets to a role in which movement on land and in water were the only means of expression. But what must have set him apart from other contenders was his height. At six feet, five inches, he was tall enough to make any monster look threatening. Frank took his punishment pretty well. But I've often wondered whether some of the Fish Man's on-screen savagery didn't grow out of Frank's resentment of those grueling makeup sessions.

Ted and I had plenty of opportunity to observe this savagery close up, since our work didn't end when the suit was finished. We were assigned to ride herd on it throughout the production, to help Frank into and out of it, to make sure he didn't try to sit down in it, and to repair any minor damage it might sustain in the course of filming. This meant that we had to be on the set with him while his scenes were being shot. But this was less interesting than it sounds. The scenes were seldom shot in chronological order, so they made little dramatic sense to begin with. And after the actors ran through them two or three times, they were drained of even that. But for sheer mind-numbing dullness they couldn't begin to compare with the periods between, while the crew set up for the next shot.

Still, the experience was not without its bright spots, and the brightest of these was Eve Capulet. Eve was our leading lady and the Fish Man's love interest. She was also about the prettiest little thing that ever put on a bathing suit, which our script gave her ample opportunity to do. All leading ladies are pretty. But Eve was also very sweet and friendly to everyone, and not all leading ladies are that. Not many of them would deign to notice the poor makeup men, but Eve came to see us on the very first day. It was Frank who brought her to us. He came up to us with Eve on one arm and his second head under the other.

"Eve is really impressed with the suit," he told us after making introductions. "She's been asking all kinds of questions about it. I know when I'm in over *my* head, so I brought her along to see the boys who built it."

"You brought her to the right place," I said, stepping forward. "Miss Capulet, I'm at your service. Just tell me what you want to know."

But all I got for my offer was a polite smile. She turned from me to Ted.

"Frank tells me *you* invented it," she said. "Where do you come up with ideas like that?"

For a moment I almost hated him. I *would* have hated him if he hadn't looked so trapped and unhappy, like a deer caught in headlights. Poor Ted! The attention of a pretty girl was something new in his life, and he didn't know which way to turn. This should have come as no surprise. In the two years we had worked together I had never heard him talk about women, and I had always figured it was because he couldn't have much to tell. As I said before, he was nobody's idea of handsome. But I had never realized until that moment just how bad off the poor guy was. It was all he could do not to bolt.

Eve caught on pretty quickly to what the trouble was, and she did what she could to help him through it. She kept him focused on the subject under discussion as if it were the most interesting thing in the world. And I have to say, her approach worked. In no time at all she had old Ted eating out of her hand, explaining the mysteries of hooks and zippers, rubber and paint as well as I've ever heard it done. They went on like that for a quarter of an hour, while Frank and I just stood there looking foolish. They went on right up to the moment Eve was called to take her place before the camera.

"I want to thank you, Ted, for giving me so much of your time. It's been very interesting. Thanks."

She smiled and held out her hand to him. He took it without hesitation.

"Thank *you*, Eve," he said. "The pleasure was all mine."

She smiled again and ran off, leaving Ted looking dumbly after her. Clearly, she had made an impression on him. But that was to be expected. Half the crew was in love with her. I was a little in love with her myself. But none of us would have thought that this meant anything. We would have understood that what had passed between Ted and Eve was nothing more than the momentary camaraderie of two people thrown briefly together by their common livelihood. I would have thought that Ted understood this too. But Ted saw things differently from the rest of us. I wouldn't know how differently until a few days later.

We were on the lake that doubled for the Amazonian lagoon, shooting a long sequence in which Eve's character goes for a swim. She stood a moment on the deck of the boat, looking stunning in her white bathing suit. She dived over the side and struck out through the water with strong and graceful strokes. She went through a number of aquatic gyrations. She swam back to the boat again. Not very exciting stuff, at least not when viewed from shore twenty yards away. But Ted saw a lot more in it than I did.

"It's beautiful, Dave," he said in an awed whisper. "We can't see him, but the Fish Man is down there too, swimming a few feet beneath her. He's too shy to touch her, too drawn by her to pull away. So he swims beneath her on his back, mirroring her every move in a beautiful courtship dance."

I was too surprised to answer him. And yet, I thought, why should I be surprised? Half the crew was in love with Eve, so why not Ted? But wasn't it ironic that this ugly man, whom no self-respecting woman would ever look at twice, should nevertheless have an advantage over the rest of us. That he alone could carry on a vicarious romance with the girl of his dreams, through the person of the monster of his imagination.

Ted didn't notice my silence. He was too caught up in thoughts of his own. When he spoke again, it was in a voice almost too soft for me to hear.

"If the picture has a heart, this is it."

I had reason to remember this a few days later. Word got out that the producers were unhappy with the underwater sequences as they appeared in the dailies. Frank Sellers might be a strong swimmer, but he was evidently not strong enough to make a good showing while encumbered with a thick layer of foam rubber. He did well enough swimming right-side up, but when, as in Ted's beloved water ballet, he had to swim upside down, the effect was downright ludicrous. "Somebody call a lifeguard!" was one screener's brutal summation. The bottom line was that the scene must be redone or dropped altogether.

Ted was so upset by this rumor that he stopped the Old Man on his way to his office. "Is it true what they're saying, sir? That the water ballet is being cut?"

The Old Man frowned and shook his head. "It looks that way, Ted. Unless we can find a way to fix it, and I don't see how we can do that. Even if we had the resources to build a new suit, we don't have a swimmer to build it for. And there would be no assurance that the new man could maneuver in it any better than the old one."

"Let *me* fix it, sir."

The Old Man was genuinely surprised by this. "Ted, I know how much this project means to you—"

"I can *do* it. I can have our new Fish Man here ready to shoot on Friday morning. But you've got to give me the chance."

The Old Man looked thoughtfully at the younger one. "Okay, Ted. You get your chance. Have your Fish Man on the lagoon set on Friday morning."

After the Old Man passed on I confronted Ted myself. "Are you nuts?" I asked him.

He considered this for a moment. "No, Dave, I don't think so."

"Well, think again. You heard what the Old Man said. Where are you going to find a swimmer who can *wear* the suit, let alone *swim* in it? You sure as hell can't build another one between now and Friday."

I have to say, he took it calmly. "You may be right. All the same, be on the lagoon set on Friday morning."

Ted didn't report to work the next day or the next, which left me with my hands full. These were Frank's last days on the shoot, and they included two of his most important scenes: the girl's rescue from the Fish Man's grotto, and the monster's subsequent death in the hail of her rescuers' bullets. These were also the last two days of primary filming, which meant that on Friday Ted would have the production unit pretty much to himself. It also meant that I would be free to go down to the lagoon set and get a look at what he had come up with.

He must have come up with something, because I arrived to find Eve already in the water, running through the gyrations of her lonely swim routine. No cameras were visible, since the scene was being played for the benefit of the underwater cameras only. I saw Ted standing beside his old van on the far side of the lake, watching like the rest of us. I couldn't get closer to him while the shoot was going on. However, I saw Frank Sellers standing in civilian clothes a few feet away from me. So I approached him and asked how things were going.

"Pretty well," he told me. "Old Ted got his Fish Man, all right. He drove up with him in the back of his van about two hours ago. The new guy—Ted introduced him as his uncle Asa—is smaller than me, and his coloring is a little lighter, but in everything else he's identical. He's not very friendly, though."

"No?"

"No. I went up to him before the shooting began, to introduce myself and compliment him on his costume. The son of a bitch just glared at me!"

Before he could tell me anything more, our attention was drawn back to action on the set. The filming had stopped. The director was walking down to the edge of the lagoon where the divers were standing chest-high in the water, giving him thumbs up. They had got what they needed, they seemed to be saying, and it looked good. Eve was being helped out of the water and into a robe and slippers. But where was the Fish Man?

"There he is," said Frank beside me. "He's coming out now."

And so he was. Nobody helped him out of the water, but he didn't seem to need it. A moment later he stood on the shore, gasping and dripping. Now that I was getting a good look at him, I realized that Frank had been a little harsh in his assessment. Asa and Frank were certainly *not* identical. The new Fish Man was superior to the old one in every way that counted. But Frank had been right about one thing. Asa didn't share his easy professionalism. Frank might be the Fish Man while the camera was rolling, but afterwards he would take off the head and make jokes about it with the crew. Asa took it more seriously. I don't think I ever saw him out of character, and I know I never saw him out of the head.

Frank wasn't the only one that this attitude rubbed the wrong way. Eve had always gotten along well with Frank, in and out of costume. But Asa seemed to make her anxious and unhappy. As soon as she noticed him standing by her, she turned without a word and hurried to her trailer. As for Asa, he just stood there looking dumbly after her, much as Ted had done under similar circumstances a week before. He stood like that until Ted came up and led him back to the van.

The director had been crouching on the shore, conferring with the divers in the water. He must have been satisfied with what they told him, because now he came up and called everyone to their places for the next shot. This was the big abduction scene, where the monster leaps off the boat with the girl in its arms and carries her down to its underwater lair. Asa and Eve reappeared from their van and trailer and took their places on the deck. Asa looked the same as ever, but Eve had changed from her white bathing suit into white shorts and a red print blouse. Her dark hair was still a little damp from her swim, but this didn't matter since the only cameras were in the water. She seemed less nervous than at the end of the last shot. But I noticed that she still kept her distance from Asa.

Then the call for action came, and Asa threw his finny arms around Eve's waist and threw them both over the side and into the water where the cameramen were waiting. Nobody but the cameramen saw what happened then, but less than a minute later Eve broke the surface alone and let out a terrified scream. I had heard actresses scream before when their roles called for it, but never like that. Everyone who heard it was as alarmed by it as I was. Three crew members jumped into the water fully clothed to get her out of there. She didn't scream again, but she was sobbing hysterically as they helped her ashore.

"Keep it away from me!" she said over and over. "Just keep it away from me!"

Asa came ashore behind them and stood there looking after them, his masked face frozen in a bug-eyed alien frown. The crew members looked at him in anger and disgust. "Somebody ought to teach that guy some manners," I heard Frank say in a low voice beside me. I guess that summed up how we all felt. But I noticed that all of us kept our distance.

Ted was in the first wave of those who had rallied to Eve's side. I saw him break away from the crowd just as Frank and I were coming up to join it. He didn't speak to us, or we to him. He didn't look like he wanted to be spoken to. He went straight to where Asa was standing and ordered him into the van. Then the two of them drove away.

I could understand how Ted must be feeling. I mean, to put so much of himself into a project he felt so strongly about, and then to have it blow up in his face, that had to hurt. And to have his beloved Eve get caught in the explosion, that had to hurt like hell. I thought more than once in the course of the day that I should give him a call and find out how he was doing. But I always decided against it. He was big enough to handle his own problems, and I would hear all about it on Monday morning. But late that night the phone rang, and I answered it to find Ted himself on the line.

"Hello, Dave. I'm sorry to break into your evening like this, but I couldn't think of anyone else to call. I want to ask you about Eve. Is she all right?"

"Yeah, she's all right. She had a bit of a scare, as you know. But by the time you left she was recovering from it nicely. You mustn't blame yourself, Ted. It isn't your fault that your uncle got a little too deep into his character. Is he there now?"

"He's in the bathtub. He can't hear me out here. But, Dave, it *is* my fault. Though God knows I never meant for anything bad to happen, to Eve or anyone. I only wanted to save the picture. It was so important to me, saving the picture, and I could see no other way to do it. But they're not like us, Dave. They're wild and dangerous. And they don't mix well with humans."

"What are you talking about, Ted? *Who* doesn't mix well with humans?"

"Listen, Dave. You know the premise of the Fish Man story, the idea that our world was once inhabited by a race of beings half man, half fish? Well, what if I told you that it's true? What if I told you that there really *was* such a race, not limited to the backwaters of the Amazon, but spread over the oceans of the prehistoric world? And what if I told you that they're still there today?"

"Ted, I—"

"Just hear me out, Dave. This is no fantasy. It isn't even much of a secret. Plenty of people have known about them for years. There are any number of fine old New England families that have made their fortunes trading with them. And some of those families have engaged in more than trade. Families like mine. Like mine and Uncle Asa's.

"You see, Dave, I wasn't kidding when I told you that I drew my Fish Man from life. Asa really is my uncle. But he's also a creature like the one in my drawing. His home is in the sea, but he can still venture out on the dry land when the need arises. It was lucky that my design was accepted, because nothing else could have enabled me to produce a double on such short notice. But it was *un*-lucky too, for the same reason.

"Because there's been a complication. It seems Uncle Asa is quite taken with Eve. Well, I can hardly blame him for that. But he wants to do more than just admire her. He wants to take her back home with him. I've tried to tell him how impossible it is, but he won't listen to me. That doesn't leave me with a lot of choices. I'm going to kill him, Dave, if I can. And I want you to know,

*The state of the front door had hardly prepared me for what I saw when I managed to turn on a light. The place was a wreck. It looked like the set of a western saloon after the big fight. Lamps were broken, chairs overturned, upholstery slashed. The carpet was soaked with water, and something else that looked like blood. And where were Ted and his uncle?*

if anything happens—"

That was as much as I could take. "Now *you* listen to *me*, Ted," I said. "This is crazy talk. You've been working too hard, or drinking too hard, or both. You don't want to kill your uncle. You want to go to bed and get some sleep. I'll come down first thing tomorrow and we'll talk about it over breakfast—"

But he had hung up.

I decided I had better not wait for morning. I headed out for his place right away. But when I pulled up in front of his bungalow about an hour later, I thought I had made the trip for nothing. The house was as dark as if he had taken my advice and gone to bed. But then I saw that the front door was open, hanging half off its hinges.

The state of the front door had hardly prepared me for what I saw when I managed to turn on a light. The place was a wreck. It looked like the set of a western saloon after the big fight. Lamps were broken, chairs overturned, upholstery slashed. The carpet was soaked with water, and something else that looked like blood. And where were Ted and his uncle?

Ted had sounded pretty crazy on the phone, but had he been crazy enough to attack his uncle under the delusion that he was a monster threatening the woman he loved? Had he been crazy enough to kill him, to drag his body out on the beach, to bury it in the sand or cast it adrift on the water? I didn't know, and it wasn't my job to find out. I dug Ted's phone out from under the wreckage and put in a call to the police. Then I went out on the porch to wait for them.

And it was there that I saw something to make me think that maybe poor old Ted hadn't been so crazy after all. Someone had gone out this way before me, tracking water and blood from the soggy carpet across the wooden deck. But that someone wasn't Ted. I knew the feet that had made the tracks, because I had spent many hours trying to duplicate their features in rubber and paint.

They were the webbed and taloned feet of the thing Ted had brought up from the sea to save his picture, the terrible thing he had called his uncle Asa.

# THE BIG PICTURE

Nothing draws a crowd like a crowd, Tom thought. Set half a dozen people to look at something on a busy street in the middle of the day, and soon there will gather twice that number just to see what they are looking at. But when Tom joined the gawkers and got a good look at the object of their gawking, he wondered if they had all conspired to make him the butt of a practical joke.

The center of attention was a street vendor's cart with a large display of cheaply framed art prints. It was the prints that the people were looking at. And not just looking. They were staring at them with an intensity of interest that could not have been matched by the most pretentious connoisseur. This would have been ridiculous even if the prints had been worth seeing. But they were not. They were the worst sort of abstractionist trash: blurry patterns of vibrating colors that defied the eye to find anything of interest there.

"It's called a stereogram," Tom heard a man say helpfully to his woman companion. "There's a 3D picture hidden inside, and you can see it if you know how to look. The trick is to unfocus your eyes, to stare at the picture like you're trying to see behind it. . . ."

The explanation continued at some length. Tom was pretty sure now that the man was in on the joke. But he had already made a fool of himself by looking, and he would not be made any more foolish by looking a little closer. He followed the man's instructions as well as he could, trying to see past the surface of the picture. For a moment nothing happened. Then the picture doubled, and the two copies slid over each other like glass transparencies. Then the transparencies snapped together in an unexpected way, and the hidden image jumped out at him. The image itself was not very impressive, a poor replica of the Great Sphinx seemingly modeled out of crumpled Christmas wrappings. But it looked so real that Tom felt he could reach out and touch it.

"Wonderful!" he said aloud to no one in particular.

"Childish!" a voice answered close behind him.

Tom pulled himself free of the spell of the picture long enough to turn and face the speaker. This was a little old man in a long black coat. The coat was buttoned to his chin in spite of the warm day. His vulture head, naked except for a few carefully brushed strands of lank black hair, was set low between his hunched shoulders. He was looking not at Tom but at one of the pictures on the cart, with a sour expression on his sharp-featured face.

"What did you say?" Tom asked.

"It's childish!" the old man repeated, without even looking to see whom he was addressing. "It's childish to hunt for worthless images in patterns of colored ink, while the great book of life lies open before us, while the secrets of the universe await our reading in the patterns of the visible world—"

The old man stopped suddenly, as if surprised to hear his own voice speaking such thoughts aloud. He turned and looked searchingly into the face of his questioner. Then he turned again and hurried off without a word. Tom's last sight of him was of his bent black form hobbling like a crippled bird along the base of a brownstone wall.

The print was light enough to carry but large enough to make it awkward. It was also unwrapped, which meant that it drew curious stares from the people Tom passed on the street. But in spite of these things he managed to get his purchase back to the office without serious mishap. He stood it on the floor against the wall of his cubicle and was just stepping back to admire it when Jack, his supervisor, stuck his head in the door.

"Hello, Tom. I just stopped by to— What the hell is that?"

"Oh, hello, Jack. That's just something I picked up after lunch. It's called a stereogram." And he launched into the explanation he had overheard in the street. But he did not get far before the other cut him off.

"You can tell me about it later. I just stopped by to thank you for all the long hours you put in on the Moreton project. It hasn't gone unnoticed. Oh yes, and to warn you that you'd better get rested up while you have the chance. We just got the go-ahead on the Phillips job, and we'll have to hit the ground running if we're going to meet the deadline."

Tom was glad when the other had gone and he could go back to admiring his picture. Well, not admiring it exactly. He was frankly puzzled by his purchase, and he was trying to understand the impulse that had led him to make it. What was the source of his sudden fascination? Surely not the picture itself. It was interesting for its novelty, but no more so than, for example, the View-Master he had played with as a child. And as for the old man, his comment showed that he was just another lunatic prophet in a city that had too many of them already.

But if neither words nor picture were alone enough to wake Tom's sudden interest, what might they be *together?* Picture and words were two sides of a single coin. Without the other each was meaningless, but together they might make up a third thing that was full of meaning, that pointed to another thing more meaningful still. After all, what had the old man really said? Not that the picture contained the secrets of the universe. That would have been crazy indeed. He had only suggested that the picture might *point the* way to those secrets. For the picture was more than a picture. It was a symbol for something larger than itself. It was a metaphor for the world.

It was all so simple once you had the key! On the surface the picture was chaotic. But to the eye that looked beneath the surface, the seeming chaos came together to reveal the secret image it contained. Was the world any different? Throughout history man had tried to discover an order in the chaos of his existence. Superstition and science were the instruments of his search. But always those instruments had failed him. Superstition had failed because it turned its back on the real world. Science had failed because it concentrated on the minutiae of that world at the expense of the big picture. Science did not guess that the big picture existed. But it did exist. It must. It was hidden, that was all, hidden like the stereogrammatic Sphinx in the pattern of the visible world. And like the Sphinx, it needed only a trained eye to discover it.

"Oh, Tom!" said Marcia, his wife, meeting him at the door a few evenings later with a new print under his arm. "Not *another* one?"

"I'm sorry, Marcia. But it's like I said before: I need them for a new project we're starting at work. I'd love to tell you about it, but you know how impatient you are with technical explanations. Anyway, it won't be for much longer."

Marcia shook her head as she stalked out of the room. But there was really nothing she could say to his lie, as Tom had foreseen when he devised it. He felt more than a little guilty about it. Still, it was easier to tell her a lie she could understand, than a truth he only partly understood himself.

Yet the truth was simple enough. How did you go about training your eyes to find the image hidden in the visible world? By exercising them with examples. If you could master the pictures where there were known images to be found and known rules for finding them, you could work your way up to wider vistas where images and rules were still unknown.

Of course Tom's progress was helped by the fact that the stereograms were becoming a full-blown fad. Otherwise the available stock must have been too limited for his purpose. Already the first cart on the open street had been joined by two others in the local malls. The pictures were given prominent display in every art and poster shop. Every book store had several volumes devoted to them. Tom could spend whole weeks of lunch hours in hunting them down and still be no closer to exhausting the supply.

Still, it could not go on much longer. On that point at least he had told the truth. The supply of stereograms might be endless, but at bottom they were all the same, and he needed variety and depth. Lately he had tried to fill his need with pictures of other kinds. Pictures of seemingly solid figures that on closer examination dissolved in a riot of disparate elements. Pictures whose elements were so arranged that they startled the viewer with unexpected faces. But when he found himself devoting more and more time to his search and turning up less and less, he knew that he had learned as much as the pictures could teach him. It was time to apply what he had learned.

He began in a small way, not because he was too timid to attempt anything larger, but because he was not yet able to conceive of anything larger to attempt. His training had so far been limited to abstract designs. Therefore, to apply his training, he logically turned to the abstract designs that occurred in his own surroundings. This proved to be a surprisingly rich field, even in the scope of his narrow life. There were suitable abstractions to be found in the austerity of a bare wall or the roughness of a textured ceiling, in the pattern of a carpet or the design of a co-worker's tie. He could stare at these for hours at a time, trying to trace the single thread that would lead him to the hidden image he sought.

But such abstractions were as limited in their scope as the pictures had been. Sooner or later he would have to expand his field of study to encompass the visible world itself. Yet this presented problems of its own. He had read enough on the psychology of perception to know that what one sees is largely shaped by what one expects to see. His own expectations had been shaped by a lifetime of seeing the same world others saw. This could only interfere with the kind of perception he wanted now. Therefore he must learn to separate the meaning from the sight. He must learn to break down the world around him into an abstract of color and texture, with no regard for body or shape.

This was easier in theory than in practice. Yet there were moments, however brief, when he felt that he really could dissolve the world around him, and reduce it to an abstract pattern as seemingly meaningless as any stereogrammatic print. Sometimes, when he had been looking hard at a particular arrangement of objects, he would see those objects begin to tremble and dissolve. At such times he felt that he was on the verge of a great discovery. But then his tired eyes would blink and change their focus, and the world would grow solid again.

Tom looked up to see his supervisor standing in the entrance of his cubicle.

"I'm sorry, Jack. Did you say something?"

"I said, how's the new draft coming? Will it be out on time?"

"It doesn't look that way. I'm having to recheck some figures, and it's taking longer than I expected. But it'll be out tomorrow for sure."

The other's face grew stern.

"That's what you said yesterday. And the day before. But every time I look in here I see you staring off into space. What's the matter, Tom? Have you forgotten how much is riding on this proposal?"

"No, Jack, I haven't forgotten. That's why it's taking so long. I want everything to be perfect."

"Perfect, huh? Just the same, I'm going to buy us some extra insurance. I'm putting Alan on the project with you. I expect you to give him your full cooperation."

*Sometimes, when he had been looking hard at a particular arrangement of objects, he would see those objects begin to tremble and dissolve. At such times he felt that he was on the verge of a great discovery. But then his tired eyes would blink and change their focus, and the world would grow solid again.*

It was strange to think how large a difference a little time could make. A month ago this scene would have upset him greatly. But now he was beyond all that. Now he saw that pain and pleasure, victory and defeat were all a matter of perception. And even the gravest of professional setbacks might serve to advance him in his *real* career. It was not good to be spending so much time at the office. The patterns did not change there. The arrangement of furniture and books varied little from day to day. The ceiling tiles remained the same no matter how long you studied them.

It was better in the street. The patterns there were always changing. You could walk for hours in any direction without encountering a sign or building you had ever seen before. But even the most familiar ways were never the same twice. For always the pattern of parked and moving cars, of standing and milling pedestrians, varied unceasingly. Always the pattern of light and shadow changed throughout the day, as the sun rose or set over the city, as it sailed across the clear blue sky or struggled through the lowering clouds. At night the headlights wove a pattern of their own, and the great grids of high-rise windows twinkled like the stars.

"Your office called today," said his wife, meeting him at the door. "They asked me where you were. They said you haven't been in all week."

"What did you tell them?" he asked without much interest.

"What *could* I tell them? That I saw you off to work every morning? That as far as I knew you were there right now? I told them you were sick. Where *were* you, Tom?"

"I went for a walk, that's all. I had some thinking to do."

"You had some thinking to do. And what did you think about, on your walk? Did you think about how we're going to pay the bills when you get fired? Tom, what's happening to you? You used to be so solid. Now you walk around in a cloud and let everything around you go to hell. What is it? Is it drugs? Is it another woman? I only wish it were. Those are things I would know how to deal with. But these damned pictures of yours—"

"Marcia, I—"

"Look at them! There's barely an inch of wall that isn't covered with them. And why? They aren't even nice to look at. For months now I've stood quietly by while you turned our home into some kind of crazy art museum. But I won't stand for it any more. You hear me? I won't stand for it any more!"

"What do you want me to do?"

"Get rid of them. Every last one of them. I'm not kidding this time. Either they go or I do."

It was a shame, really, for he loved her in his way. And it was not as if the pictures were worth holding onto. He had only kept them around to help him focus his thoughts, and lately they had not been useful even for that. It was a long time since the scope of his experiment could be contained within the boundaries of a few cheap picture frames. It had broken free of them months ago, and spilled out into the world around him just as the pictures had spilled out over the walls. He had outgrown them. But Marcia was a distraction, as his job was a distraction. He was better off without them both.

What did it matter if he had no job, no wife, no home? These things were only tragedies as long as he persisted in seeing himself as an individual outside the big picture. And he was learning to let go of that. It was not an easy thing to learn. So long as he was flesh and blood he would be subject to the pains of hunger and loneliness and cold. But he had hopes that it would become easier as he went along. In any case, it was a lesson he had to learn, if he was to see what he wanted to see.

For he knew now that he would not truly see the big picture until he could dissolve the boundary that separated him from it, the boundary of the self. Yet after all, what was there in identity to make it worth holding onto? It was identity that kept him dependent on his surroundings, that tied him to one place and time, that set limits of birth and death on his existence. But once he gave it up, there would be no such limitations. He would take his place in the big picture. He would be one with the universe.

And then one evening he saw the old man again. It was in the decaying heart of the city, not far from where Tom had first encountered him, that he spotted his bent black form walking a little ahead of him. There was no mistaking him. It was almost a year to the day since Tom had seen him last, yet he had not changed in all that time. There was the same long black coat buttoned to the neck in spite of the warm evening. There was the naked vulture head set low between the hunched shoulders. There was the same strange hobbling gait suggestive of a crippled bird.

Tom had not thought of him for a long time, not since the earliest days of his search. But now his interest was rekindled. He had tried to teach himself to see, and failed. But what he could not teach himself, he could still be taught by another. Surely the old man had not spoken at random. Surely he already possessed the knowledge that Tom was looking for. Tom could not let him go unquestioned. He ran toward him, calling for him to wait.

The old man did not stop or turn. But he must have heard Tom just the same, for suddenly he quickened his pace. He moved so quickly that he got around the corner and halfway up a narrow alley before Tom caught up with him. But he could not have gone much farther in any case, since the alley had no other opening than the one by which they had entered.

The old man turned at bay. "Leave me alone," he whined. "I have nothing for you."

"Don't be afraid," said Tom. "I won't hurt you. I only want to talk to you."

"Talk to me?" The old man seemed less frightened now, but not less suspicious. "Why? You don't even know me."

"Yes, I do," said Tom. "We met and spoke once, long ago. Someone was selling stereograms on the street. We looked at them together, and you said they were childish. Remember?"

"I remember," said the old man, looking at the other more closely now. "You've come down in the world since then."

"You said something else, too. 'It's childish to hunt for worthless images in patterns of colored ink, while the secrets of the universe await our reading in the patterns of the visible world.' Do you remember? I do. Because it set me to thinking. About the little pictures we all see, and the big picture none of us sees, the hidden face of the universe. I decided that a man's life could have no greater purpose than to find the big picture and take up his rightful place in it. So I made up my mind to try. I devoted all my waking hours to the attempt. It cost me my job, my home, my wife. But I don't care about that. I'd give them up all over again to find what I'm looking for."

"What has this to do with me?"

"It has *everything* to do with you. It was you who put me on the trail, so you must know where it leads. So you and you alone must be able to teach me how to see. You can do it, can't you?"

The old man was silent for a moment, thinking, thinking. "Yes, I can teach you," he said at last. But before Tom could begin to thank him, he went on:

"I can teach you. But are you sure you want to learn? It may not be quite what you expect, you know. One cannot look on the face of God and not be *changed* by it. The ancients knew this very well. The Hebrews forbade it outright. The Greeks embodied their prohibition in the story of the Gorgon, whose glance turns men to stone. Alhazred warns us more than once of the punishment that awaits the foolish mortal who dares to enter the court of Azathoth unbidden—"

"I'm not afraid."

"No, I don't believe you are," said the old man, looking hard into the face of the young one. "Well, let us begin. Stand just here, with your feet apart. Now cast your eye on the evening star where it shines above yonder lamppost. . . ." He gave Tom some more instructions, punctuated with gestures of his claw-like hand. Then he asked, "Do you see?"

"No," said Tom.

"Look harder. Do you see now?"

"No. Yes. That is, I think I see—"

It was about this time that the peace of the neighborhood was shattered by a scream. Screams were not unusual in that district, but there was something in the tone and volume of this scream that raised the hackles of even the most hardened residents. So terrible was the sound, that they let a full minute go by before anyone went out to investigate. They arrived in time to see the black-coated figure of a stooped old man hurrying away from the scene. But they found no evidence that anything unusual had taken place. That is to say, no *visible* evidence.

But some of their number would later claim to have found evidence that was *audible*. For the first men to arrive at the entrance of the alley seemed to hear a voice speaking uncomfortably near them. The nearness was uncomfortable because there was no one there who could have spoken. There were no windows overlooking the alley, and the alley itself offered no cover for anyone to hide behind. Yet the voice was unmistakable. It seemed to be the voice of a man, but a man reduced by terror to a sort of second childhood. The sad little voice went on and on, repeating the same simple phrases over and over until it faded into silence:

"Help me. *Please* help me. Let me out. *Please* let me out. Help me. . . ."

# OMEGA

A buzzer sounded overhead, calling Walter Kessler out of a warm black oblivion. For a moment he lay there in the dark, trying to remember where he was and what the buzzer meant. When he did remember he looked at the luminous display of his wristwatch. Eight minutes to ten. Joe Murphy was early. Not early enough to be inconvenient, but enough to show his eagerness to begin. He had always been an eager student, and it was nice to see that he had lost none of his enthusiasm. But his enthusiasm would not hold him at the front door forever, not if Kessler did not get upstairs to meet him.

He unlocked the door and opened it to find a plump, bespectacled young man blinking at him in the yellow porch light.

"Dr. Kessler?"

"You know it is, Joe." Kessler smiled broadly and held out his hand. "It's good to see you again. Come in out of the cold."

He stepped aside to let Joe pass, then closed the door and locked it again behind him. When he turned around, Joe had already taken off his coat and was hanging it on a peg in the paneled wall.

"I'm glad you were able to come on such short notice. It must be a terrible inconvenience."

"Not at all. It's a rare privilege to be called on to be a part of this."

"Did you have any trouble finding the place?"

"No. Your directions were very clear." Joe looked around. "This is a wonderful old house you have here."

"Thanks. It belonged to my parents. I used to think it was too large for an old bachelor like me to rattle around in. But you'd be surprised how fast even a place like this fills up."

"You must have amassed quite a collection, after a lifetime of study and travel."

"Why, yes, I suppose I have. I hope to show you some of it before the night is over. But for now we'll go straight to the library. I've set up for us in there."

The older man laid his hand on the younger one's shoulder and guided him through the intricacies of the house. Yes, it *was* a wonderful house, he thought to himself. It was too bad that it took another's eyes to help one appreciate it, that too much familiarity dulled one's perception. It really was a showcase in its way. The furniture was old, but solid and well made. Not flashy, but with an air of prosperous respectability.

The real showcase was the library. The walls were lined with glass-fronted bookcases wherever there was room for them. Other cases, freestanding and glass-topped, displayed a small museum of archeological treasures. Two leather wingchairs were drawn up on either side of the fireplace, with a little round table set between. On the table was a tray with a decanter and two glasses. While Joe wandered over to one of the cases and looked appreciatively at its collection of chipped flints and sharpened bones, Kessler went to the table and filled the glasses from the decanter.

"You kept your coming here a secret, Joe?"

"Of course."

"Forgive me for asking. But as you probably know, most of the world believes I'm dead. When the news of my reappearance gets out there is bound to be a certain amount of media attention. And I would like to put that off for as long as possible, until I am ready to present my findings to the world. With your help, Joe. With your help."

He carried the two glasses over to Joe and handed him one.

"Let us begin our collaboration with a toast. To Hyperborea, shall we say?"

"To Hyperborea," Joe repeated, and the two men raised their glasses. But Joe's glass was only half empty when he lowered it again.

"Then it's true? You really found it?"

"Yes, Joe, I found it. Have a seat and I'll tell you about it."

Joe sat down in the chair across from Kessler. But he was too impatient to wait for the other to begin.

"I followed the story closely at the time, but I only know what I read in the papers. I know that you mounted an expedition to western Greenland to search for the remains of a prehistoric civilization, the one the ancient Greeks called Hyperborea, the country behind the north wind. I know that the expedition never returned. But that's about all. The papers said next to nothing about where you went or what started you on your search. How did you find it?"

"How does one find anything? A fortunate confluence of evidence, and the wit to see how it fits together. But here, take a look at this."

Kessler picked something up from the table beside him, a shiny black object about eight inches long. He handed it to Joe.

"That obsidian knife was my first piece of evidence. I found it six years ago in a cave in northern Italy. Examine it closely. Observe how beautifully shaped it is, how finely finished, how perfectly preserved. Obviously, a thing like that had no place in the typical Neolithic household. Such things turn up from time to time in archeological digs. Cultural anomalies, we call them. Artifacts which, if not exactly beyond the technology of a people to produce, yet stand so far apart from their other productions that they *must* have been introduced from without. So they are dismissed as the result of modern contamination, and shelved away as scientific embarrassments. Just as that knife would have been shelved away, except for one of those confluences of evidence I mentioned earlier.

"My next piece of evidence did not appear until some years later. Four years later, to be exact. That was when the University library acquired its copy of the *Book of Eibon*."

Joe looked up from the knife he was holding. "The *Book of Eibon*?"

"You haven't heard of it? I'm not surprised. It has always been more the province of occultists than of real scientists. It is undeniably old, being directly traceable to a ninth-century Latin text. But it purports to be even older, to trace its descent back to ancient Egypt, and to Atlantis before that, and beyond Atlantis through unnumbered eons to Hyperborea itself. A pedigree like that, even a false one, is enough to pique anyone's interest. Of course the book is impossibly rare and its access severely restricted. But even the severest restrictions can be gotten around with the right credentials, and it was not long before I was permitted to see for myself what all the excitement was about.

"At first I was not impressed. The book was of interest only as a fantasy. But what a fantasy! The tale of a mighty empire that rose and fell before the last ice age, on a jungle continent roughly corresponding to modern Greenland. An empire of mighty cities with gorgeous names like Commorium and Uzuldaroum, rising in barbaric splendor in the shadow of Voormithadreth itself. Voormithadreth was Hyperborea's sacred mountain, the holiest place in the prehistoric world. Its holiness derived from the belief that it was the preeminent hive or fortress of the Hyperborean gods. Here in its caverns were said to dwell the toad-like Tsathoggua, the spidery Atlach-Nacha and, greatest of all, the formless Ubbo-Sathla, the ultimate source and predestined end of all life on earth. And here, until the great ice whelmed Hyperborea's cities and drove its gods to seek a friendlier clime deeper underground, their human priests maintained their temples and their shrines, supported by offerings from their worshippers on the plain below.

"But I was not *really* impressed until I found something else within its pages. Until I found a mark like a circle under an inverted V with four points instead of one. The circle that signifies the proliferating womb and the devouring mouth, the dual aspects of godhood. The V that signifies the fortress of the Hyperborean gods themselves, the mountain of four volcanic cones that the Hyperborean people called Voormithadreth. The circle and V that are exactly reproduced on the base of my obsidian blade!

"You can imagine my excitement. I had no faith in Eibon alone, but Eibon and the knife together were powerful arguments. The knife was an anomaly still, but its connection to Eibon suggested that it had been introduced not through any *modern* contamination but through an exceedingly *ancient* one. Eibon's book was no less fantastic, but the existence of the knife suggested that it was less a myth than a veracious history. Besides, what did I have to refute them? Greenland may be a frozen waste today, but a million years ago it was warm enough to support a civilization.

"The only question was, where to look for it? Hyperborea's legendary cities are buried deep under permanent glacial ice. We can pluck down rocks from the moon more easily than we can find the least brick or tile from the palaces of the Hyperborean kings. But mountains are another matter. However deep under the ice the remains of that civilization might be buried, its sacred mountain must still stand over it. Voormithadreth was the place to look for evidence of the Hyperborean culture.

"The rest was relatively simple. I made a survey of the available aerial and satellite maps of modern Greenland. And it was here that I found my third and final piece of evidence. I found, in the mountainous region that runs along the western coast, a configuration of four round volcanic craters grouped close together, like the paw print of some gigantic beast impressed in stone for all time. A configuration that exactly matched old Eibon's description of Voormithadreth. Careful, Joe! You'll cut yourself. That edge is very sharp."

Joe looked reproachfully at the obsidian blade in his hand. Then he passed it back to Kessler. "Maybe you'd better take charge of this," he said. "I'm not at my best tonight. The wine seems to have gone straight to my head."

"Relax and enjoy it," Kessler suggested. "This is something of an occasion for both of us. We're *supposed* to be a little high." But he returned the knife to its place on the table.

"Well, I had found my mountain. Schleimann himself had no better proof when he set out in search of buried Troy. But even he might have had trouble getting funding for his expedition nowadays. I certainly was not able to interest the University in funding mine. Fortunately I had enough money to pay my own way, and enough reputation to convince three others to join me. These were Adrian Blair, a colleague of mine, and two graduate students, Matt Reed and Tony Cernek.

"We went out that very summer. A series of commercial flights took us as far as Godthåb on the southwestern Greenland coast. A chartered helicopter took us the rest of the way, north and east across the mountains to the one I had identified, and to our campsite on the glacier at the foot of its southern slope. We spent the rest of the day setting up camp, and then a restless night waiting for morning so that we could begin our search in earnest.

"We had no clear idea of what we were searching *for*. The only thing we felt sure of was that we would not find it in the open. However many roads and temples had been here once, they could not have stood up to the constant scouring of wind and ice for three quarters of a million years. The best we could hope for was some minor shrine hidden away in some sheltered nook or cranny. Therefore our approach was to work our way around the mountain's lower slopes, investigating such caves and fissures as came within our reach. The work was long and hard, since there were rather a lot of these caves and fissures, and only a few of them were easy to get to. And not one of them held anything to make it worth our while. But archeologists are nothing if not patient. However unproductive our search was now, we had every hope that it would be rewarded in the future.

"And then it *was* rewarded, in a manner beyond anything we could have hoped for. Toward the end of the second day Tony Cernek came running into camp in wild-eyed excitement, yelling about some amazing discovery he had made. The rest of us were cold and tired after a hard day's work, but not so cold and tired that we did not immediately turn out again to see what he was yelling about. The idiot would not tell us what he had found. He kept insisting that we see it for ourselves. But we knew from his excitement that it must be something big.

"It was big all right. Tony had been right not to tell us. Nothing could have prepared us to see the thing except the thing itself. Nothing else could have prepared us to see, at the back of an icy shelf between two big piers of stone, that great square doorway carved out of the living rock in imitation of post and lintel. And now we knew why Tony had insisted that we bring lanterns. For behind the doorway was a cave or tunnel penetrating deep into the heart of the mountain. We could not think of sleep after that. We could not think of anything but to plunge in at once and start examining our find.

"Our examination started with the tunnel itself. It was pretty impressive in its own right. It was cut with wonderful precision through the hard volcanic rock, in a feat of engineering that would be hard to equal even today. The floor and ceiling were perfectly smooth, but the walls were ornamented with series of shallow niches cut into them at regular intervals. They seemed to have been intended as shrines of some sort, maybe to hold statues of the Hyperborean gods. The statues were all gone now, carried off by the departing priests or the robbers who came after them. But what might be left further down?

"For the tunnel was just the beginning. Its far end opened onto a natural cave. The walls and ceiling were seemingly untouched, but the floor was cut into a series of wide terraces and narrow stairs to smooth our passage downward. That was the direction the cave now took us, downward and inward toward the core of the mountain, growing wider and deeper at every step of the way. Probably it was a lesser branch of one of the four main volcanic vents. Maybe it would continue forward until it joined one. Indeed, at one point we thought it had. The ceiling and walls flew up and back until they were lost in darkness, and the floor fell away beneath our feet so that it was lost in darkness too.

"That would have been the end of it. Except that there was another road before us, a road in the shape of a wide causeway of loose-laid stones leading across the abyss. It looked solid enough for a structure as old as it must have been, though we would have trusted ourselves to something less solid if it would have gotten us to the other side. But we had not followed it more than a hundred feet when we found that it was not as solid as it had appeared. Part of it had been shaken down by some violent seismic upheaval, so that all that remained was a kind of ragged stair descending into darkness. For a moment we stopped at the head of this stair, debating how to proceed. But our course was never really in doubt. We were poised at the threshold of a whole new world, a world of unknown peoples and unknown gods, calling to us across the gulf of three quarters of a million years. It would take more than the prospect of a little rock climbing to make us turn back now.

"We climbed down the stair to where it disappeared under a slope of rubble. Then we climbed down over the rubble slope to find the cavern floor. Above the floor the slope leveled off into a long mound that continued the line of the broken causeway. We followed along the top of this mound in the hope that it would eventually turn up again to rejoin the causeway on the other side. I say hope, because we had no better way of knowing where it would lead us. We certainly could not see that far. Our lanterns were powerful enough to light us over the stones, but they could not do much more than that. They were useless to pierce the heavy darkness that closed us in on every side.

"How shall I describe that darkness? I had never before appreciated the powerful effect that unrelieved darkness and silence can have on the human mind. It was as if the brain tried to see and hear what the eyes and ears could not. I could understand now why the first men to come here had thought they had discovered the anteroom of hell. I could understand why they had peopled it with monsters, with gods that were half devils and devils that were half gods. Black, toad-like Tsathoggua, crouching sleepily under the stone. Spidery Atlach-Nacha, spanning unfathomable abysses with innumerable bridges of silk. And Ubbo-Sathla, the father and mother of all earthly life, sloughing from its shapeless sides the endless waves of its shapeless spawn. Sending those spawn into the world, to grow and multiply and slowly evolve into every kind of animal and plant. Calling them back at the end of days to be absorbed again.

"At last our long trek was approaching its end. At last we were on the upward slope that would take us back to the causeway. But it was here that Matt Reed made a discovery of his own. He had stopped a little ahead of us while he shone his light farther up the slope to try to find the top. Suddenly he turned back to us and told us in a low, tense voice to shine our lights in the same direction. Of course we did as he instructed. Imagine our elation when we saw, by the combined beams of our lanterns, a black cliff rising forty feet above us, a black cliff crowned with what appeared to be the standing ruins of some human habitation! Then imagine our chagrin when, lowering our beams a little farther, we saw the cliff fall sheer for twenty feet to the highest point of the stony slope.

"Blair and the others were too excited by the ruins to be put off by a mere cliff. They were soon making plans to get us to the top. But I was not so hopeful. Besides, by this time it had occurred to me, as it had not done in the first excitement of our find, that we already had more than enough to justify a full-scale expedition. So I decided to take immediate steps to put that expedition together. But to do this I had to return to camp and the radio. I called to Blair to tell him where I was going. He nodded absently in response. I wonder now if he even heard me. My last sight of him was of him standing under the great black wall, playing the circle of his lantern over its unscaleable face.

"Back in camp I had no trouble raising our agent in Godthåb. But the rest was not so easy. It would have been hard enough just trying to persuade my department head to send us reinforcements. But I had to try to find him first, and at the height of summer too. In the end the best I could do was leave him a message with little hope that it would accomplish either. Then I started back to rejoin my companions.

"There is no real night at that latitude at that time of year, though the sun passing behind the mountain had left our side deep in shadow. And the way between the camp and the door was not long enough or complicated enough to be hard to find even if it had been darker. Yet I could not find it. I went over the ground again and again without success. After several hours there was nothing left but to return to camp and radio Godthåb for help. When the helicopter arrived next day, I told the pilot that Blair and the others had been buried in an avalanche. Maybe it was true. But I didn't believe it then, and I don't believe it now. Because I remembered how we had found the door in a place where no door should have been, a place we must have passed many times in the last two days without detecting any sign of its existence. And because I saw, in the morning twilight, the marks of our boots crossing the shelf to end against a blank stone wall."

For the last several minutes Joe had appeared not to be listening. He leaned back in his chair with his eyes closed and his head resting against one of the leather wings. For all his reaction to Kessler's story, he might have been asleep. He reacted to it now, though. He pulled himself up and tried to focus on Kessler with heavy-lidded eyes.

"A blank stone wall? Is that supposed to be a joke? With all due respect, Dr. Kessler, I hope you haven't called me here just to listen to a lot of fairy tales."

"No joke, Joe, and no fairy tale either. Everything I have told you tonight is true. And before you leave I will prove it to you. Now finish your wine and we'll go."

"Go? Go where?"

"To the basement. I keep my proof down there."

The two men rose, and the older guided the younger through a doorway at the back. Their way now took them to a part of the house that was considerably less showy than the front part. It was designed for bald utility, with kitchen and pantry and other rooms whose only purpose was to maintain the comfort of the rest. Kessler hoped that Joe was not too disappointed. But Joe was in no condition to notice. Just keeping one foot in front of the other was taking up most of his attention.

"Maybe we should put this off awhile. You seem a little wobbly."

Joe shook his head. "I'm okay," he said. He did not sound okay. But he seemed determined to continue as if he were.

"There's something I'm still not clear on. You talk about proof. But I thought you never found any proof, at least none that you could carry away?"

"A fair question, Joe. There was one proof. But I did not find it until I had left my companions. My way back to camp lay over the ruined causeway, but I did not relish the thought of scrambling over its stones again so soon after the first time. I thought it would be easier to go around them, at least until I was closer to the part of the causeway that was still standing. But the stones were scattered far and wide and I had to go far and wide to avoid them, deep into the darkness and silence of the abyss.

"I had already experienced the workings of darkness and silence on the imagination. But my experience had been limited before, buffered by the company of Blair and the others. I got the full force of them now that I was alone. And yet the effect was rather subtle. I did not so much imagine monsters as consider the possibility that monsters might exist. Take Ubbo-Sathla for example. It is such a strange god to be found in the pantheon of a primitive people. It is easy to conceive of gods in the shape of toads or spiders, because toads and spiders are a natural part of the human experience. But how can one conceive of a god in the shape of a giant ameba, and declare it the foundation of the evolution of species, a million years before Leeuwenhoek and Darwin? He cannot—unless he has previously been in contact with a creature that somehow suggested both.

"It was all nonsense of course. But a moment later I came upon something that made me wonder just how nonsensical it really was. I came upon a sort of hollow in the cavern floor, a shallow depression whose gently sloping sides ran down to the edge of a circular pool about sixty feet across. I call it a pool as if it contained something liquid, but its contents had been frozen solid for three quarters of a million years. Imagine a swimming pool frozen into an opaque white mass, with a great white dome rising over the center, and you will have a pretty good idea of what it was like.

"As for me, I believed that this pool and its contents would prove to be as important as anything else we might find there. I decided to take a sample. I gouged out a lump of the frozen stuff with the point of my knife and, having nothing better on hand, scraped it into an aspirin bottle which I happened to be carrying with me."

They had reached the door of the basement. Kessler unlocked and opened it and the two men paused on the threshold. The space before them was almost completely black. The only light came from the dim bulb in the passage behind them. It lit the top of a crude flight of wooden stairs but left the rest in darkness.

"I thought that the stuff was important, but it was not until I got it back to the States that I realized *how* important. I believed that I had found something truly remarkable, something that would rewrite the book of life from its earliest chapters. But I soon learned that this was only half of it. I learned—But see for yourself."

He snapped a switch and the basement was flooded with light.

The light showed Kessler nothing that he had not seen many times before, yet he could never see it without being startled by it. The basement was drowned in a semi-liquid mass, a doughy white substance that covered the floor, the walls and the foot of the stairs to a depth of about three feet. The mass was mostly quiet, but with shiftings and heavings here and there as if something were stirring just below the surface. Maybe these were only the outward signs of an inward fermentation. But they gave the whole a furtive look, and a suggestion of sinister intelligence.

If Kessler could not see this mass without being startled, what about Joe? He had moved forward so that Kessler could no longer see his face. But he could still gauge his reaction by his tensed shoulders and craning neck, and by the way he groped downstairs for a closer view without once looking at his feet.

Halfway down he stopped and looked back at Kessler.

"I don't understand. What *is* this?"

"Steady, Joe. This is the proof I told you about. This is the sample I took from the frozen pool."

"But how did it get so *big*?"

"By eating. Its appetite manifested itself very early on. At first it ate only insects and rodents. Later it graduated to cats and dogs which I lured with food or purchased from shelters. But there is no limit to what it will eat, or to how much it will grow."

"Eat? Grow? You talk as if this stuff were alive!"

"It *is* alive, Joe. More alive than you or I. More alive than other living thing on the planet. How could it be otherwise when it is the very source of life? But remember, godhood has *two* phases. Creation *and* destruction. Birth *and* death. Proliferating womb *and* devouring mouth. The creative phase is long

*The light showed Kessler nothing that he had not seen many times before, yet he could never see it without being startled by it. The basement was drowned in a semi-liquid mass, a doughy white substance that covered the floor, the walls and the foot of the stairs to a depth of about three feet.*

since over. It ended millions of years before the Hyperboreans came, before they found the thing and gave it their worship. It was entering its destructive phase even then, so that even from their earliest beginnings its rites included animal sacrifice. Then the ice came and interrupted the cycle. It put the thing to sleep and to fast for three quarters of a million years. But now it is awake and hungry. Hungry for its children. Hungry with an appetite that cannot be sated until it has devoured every living thing on earth. That's where you come in."

"Where I—"

"Don't look so surprised, Joe. You might have guessed that you aren't the first person I brought down here. You might have guessed that the thing didn't grow as large as this on a few stray dogs and cats. The others had trouble understanding, too. Yet it is really very simple. Throughout history, man has longed to meet his creator face to face, and to merge with him in the totality of his being. Now you are about to do both.

"Any more questions? No? Then let us begin."

Kessler reached into his jacket pocket and brought out a shiny black object about eight inches long. It was the obsidian knife from the library table.

But at that instant a heavy weight slammed into his chest. And an instant later he found himself lying on his back across the steps with Joe on top of him, clutching his throat with one hand and the wrist of the hand that held the knife with the other. This was the last thing Kessler had expected. His victims had always been too doped up before, or else too cowed by Kessler's knife, to offer any real resistance. He must have misjudged this one's level of intoxication, as well as the speed and strength that had enabled him to close in a single bound the six-foot gap between them. But Kessler was strong too, and his brain was not clouded by any drug. With a single deft maneuver he broke Joe's hold and heaved him violently off. He caught a brief glimpse of him hanging in the air, arms flailing, fingers clawing at nothing, before he toppled backward and disappeared from sight.

Kessler was dazed and winded from the fight, but he could not rest until he was sure it was over. He pulled himself upright by the handrail and staggered downstairs to the last free step. He lowered himself to his haunches and leaned forward over his knees, anxiously scanning the white surface beneath him, searching for some sign of the vanished man. But there was nothing, only the ghostly reflection of his own face mirrored in the glassy calm.

Kessler closed his eyes. Everything was as it should be. His work was done—until next time. There was nothing left but to let himself sink into warm white oblivion until Ubbo-Sathla should send him forth again.

# THE MASK

If Leo had thought about what he was doing he probably would not have done it. But he did not think. The moment his headlights caught the tableau of three young white men beating up an old black one, he acted on pure instinct. He drove his pickup straight into the curb, brakes squealing, horn blaring angrily. So effective was his entrance that, when he jumped out of the cab with the tire iron in his fist, he found that the young men had all run away, leaving the old one crumpled on the sidewalk.

Leo's exhilaration over the success of his maneuver quickly gave way to concern for the condition of the fallen man. He went over and knelt beside him, examining him in the headlights. He was old and frail, maybe seventy years of age, small and slender, with skin the color of coffee and milk. He was neatly dressed in a dark suit which must have gone out of style sometime in the sixties. The white wool of his hair was stained with red.

"Are you alive, old man?" Leo asked.

The other only groaned.

"Don't worry about those punks," Leo said. "They're gone. They ran off when my truck pulled up. But they may come back when they realize there's only one of me. Come on. We'll get you out of here."

The old man did not respond. Leo helped him to his feet and half carried him to the waiting pickup. He bundled him into the cab, then got in on the other side behind the steering wheel. By the time he had backed away from the curb and pulled out into the street, his passenger had recovered enough to say:

"Where are you taking me?"

"To a doctor," said Leo in surprise and relief. "We need to get you some help. Those punks roughed you up pretty bad, and—"

"No. No doctors."

"But your head. You might have—"

"No doctors," the old man said again. "If you'll just pull over and let me out, I can walk home from here."

"Okay. If you won't let me take you to a doctor, at least let me drive you home."

The old man sat silent for a moment, considering. "All right," he said at last. "Turn left at the next corner."

For a while they drove like that, the old man speaking only to give directions, Leo following them in silence. But Leo could not restrain himself forever.

"What happened back there?"

The old man shrugged. "Just some young men looking for a little excitement. I guess they thought they'd found it in me."

"You're lucky they didn't kill you. They probably would have, if I hadn't come along when I did. What were you doing out there?"

"A man has to go out sometimes. I had some letters to send."

"In the middle of the night?"

"Sometimes night is safer."

"Well, you should be more careful. The city has really gone downhill in the last couple of years. It's the gangs mostly, fighting their lousy turf wars. Turf wars! By the time somebody wins the war, the turf won't be worth having. But I don't need to tell *you!*"

"No," the other agreed. "You don't need to tell me."

Neither of them spoke after that, so Leo went back to concentrating on his driving. But the district he was driving through was a perfect example of what he had been talking about. The place where he had rescued the old man was bad enough, but he would not have come here on a bet. It looked like a war zone. All the street lamps were dark. Many buildings were simply gone, fallen to the wrecking ball. Others were hollow, burnt-out shells waiting their turn to go.

But even the buildings that were most intact were just as dark and dead. There was one in particular that caught Leo's attention. Once it had been part of a row of brownstone tenement houses, before the lots around it were razed to the ground. Now it rose above the emptiness like a lone monument in an architectural graveyard.

"That's my building," said the old man, pointing to the dark facade.

Leo pulled up in front of it. He got out of the truck and locked it carefully, then went around to join the old man who was already standing on the curb. The latter looked at him in surprise.

"Don't say it," said Leo, raising his hand. "I didn't bring you this far just to drop you off at the curb. Somebody has to look after your wounds."

The other frowned but said nothing. Together they started up the walk to the front door. But they had not reached the bottom step before Leo began to wonder what he had let himself in for. He had thought that the windows were only dark. Now he saw that those in the ground floor were boarded up. The door, however, was slightly open.

"What do we do for light?" Leo asked, looking past the door into the darkness behind it.

"There's a lamp and a box of matches inside on the floor."

Leo found them. The lamp was of the old-fashioned kind with a tall glass chimney, and he had to fumble around a little before he managed to light it. Then he looked up into the entryway before him. He had expected to find the

*But even the buildings that were most intact were just as dark and dead. There was one in particular that caught Leo's attention. Once it had been part of a row of brownstone tenement houses, before the lots around it were razed to the ground. Now it rose above the emptiness like a lone monument in an architectural graveyard.*

inside of the building as rundown as the outside. He had not expected to find it empty. But it was stripped of everything that could be carried away. There was nothing left but a few balls of dust rolling across a scarred linoleum floor.

"We'll have to take the stairs," said the old man. "The elevator doesn't work anymore, not since the company turned off the power."

How long ago was that? Leo wondered. But he said nothing aloud. Still carrying the lamp, he followed the old man up the boxy spiral toward the darkness overhead. The climb was monotonous and slow. Monotonous, because every flight and landing was exactly like the last. Slow, because the young man had to conform himself to the careful pace of the old one. But at last it came to an end. The old man led Leo off the landing and across the hall to a certain door. He unlocked it with a key which he took from his trouser pocket.

"Excuse the mess," he said as Leo followed him in. "I'm all alone up here, and I've never been much for housework."

Leo silently agreed. The room was musty and old-fashioned, with furniture that must have been getting shabby when Leo's parents were born. The most modern piece was the TV set, and even that was an antique, a throwback to a time of large cabinets and small screens. The atmosphere was not improved by the heavy black curtains that covered the windows, shutting out light and air alike. But worst of all was the newspapers, great untidy stacks of them standing around the room, some of them so close together that it must have been hard to pass between them.

"Now," said Leo, "let's take a look at that head of yours." He put the lamp on a little table and settled the patient on a nearby couch so that he could examine his wounds. Viewed calmly in the warm interior light, they did not look severe.

"I think you'll live," Leo said presently. "At least your head has stopped bleeding. How do you feel?"

"Fine. I feel fine."

"Then I guess I'm finished here. If you have another lamp for me, I'll find my own way out."

But the old man was suddenly anxious for him to stay.

"Look here," he said. "I don't mind telling you I'm still a little shook up after what happened. I'd really appreciate it if you could sit with me awhile, just, you know, until I feel a little calmer."

"I don't know," said Leo. "It's pretty late, and I have to get up early."

"I could fix you a nice cup of coffee. It's the least I can do to repay you for your kindness."

Leo opened his mouth to refuse, then closed it again. After all, the old man had reason to be nervous after what he had been through. He was probably lonely, too.

"I guess one cup won't hurt."

"I won't be long. Make yourself at home."

The old man rose and disappeared into the next room. Leo could hear him banging around in there. He wondered how, with no utilities, his host would manage to heat his water, let alone get water to heat. But the process was bound to take a few minutes even under the best conditions. Leo decided to devote the time to a closer inspection of the things around him.

The stacks of newspapers drew his attention first. He had thought that they were only the common local variety collected for recycling. But now he saw that they were not. They were not strictly local, to begin with. They represented most of the major American cities, and more than a few foreign ones. Nor were they printed exclusively in English. The old man must be a real scholar if he could read even half the languages represented here.

But the strangest object in the room was the TV set. Leo went over to examine it more closely. It looked as if it had been put together from a kit and later repaired with improvised parts. It sat in a vicious tangle of cables and wires, like an octopus sleeping in the midst of its tentacles, or a great spider crouching in the center of its web. It appeared to be powered by a bank of maybe a dozen car batteries.

Leo knew nothing about the power requirements of TV sets, but he was pretty sure that there must be a certain amount of overkill in this arrangement. But maybe the power was needed for something more than simple reception. The thought roused his curiosity. He itched to turn the set on, but he was afraid that to do so would overstep the bounds of the old man's hospitality. Yet had not the old man invited him to make himself at home?

He turned it on. But the results were not impressive. Instead of a picture, there was only a pattern of static snow. Instead of sound, there was only an insectile whine or hum. He turned it off again.

Just then the old man reappeared with two steaming mugs on a plastic tray. He laid the tray on an improvised coffee table, a couple of cartons of old magazines, and the men sat down in two chairs on opposite sides of it. Leo picked up his coffee and tasted it. It was strong and hot the way he liked it, but with a sickly undertaste which its bitter strength could not hide. He put it down again.

"So you're all by yourself up here," he said to divert attention from his action. "It must get pretty lonely."

"Maybe it would for some people," the other replied, sipping his own coffee with obvious relish. "Me, I like it. I like having the building to myself. Oh, I admit it's no joke keeping up the place and providing for myself. On the other hand, there's nobody to take note of my comings and goings or interrupt me at my work."

"What kind of work do you do?"

"I'm what you might call a student of humanity. I study the trends of modern civilization."

"Which trends are those?"

"None you haven't heard of. One or two you have already named. The decline of cities. The rise of ignorance and crime. The division of once-great nations into many warring factions. The corruption in high places that doesn't even try to disguise itself. All the symptoms of the creeping decadence that infects our civilization like a disease."

"I see. But it seems to me that all these trends are pretty well known *without* your studying them. So what's the point?"

"Some folks would say there *is* no point. It depends on what you believe. If you believe that the fall of nations is caused by the working of natural laws as relentless as the tides, then you must think that a study like mine is a waste of time. You might as well retire to your castle of sand and watch the waves roll in. But if you believe, as I do, that it has a more localized and accessible cause, a cause that can be fought and defeated, then you must feel called upon, as I am, to arm yourself against that cause by learning as much about it as you can."

"What cause?" Leo asked.

"There's a society at work in this city today, as in all the great cities of the world. It's not a large society, though there's reason to think it's larger now than at any time in its history. But what it lacks of power in numbers, it makes up for in cunning. Its very existence is unknown to all but a very few. Its members are known only to themselves. They move undetected through all walks of life, from the highest palaces of wealth and power to the lowest slums of beggary, exerting their subtle influence everywhere. And all their exertions are carefully planned to move us closer and closer to their ultimate goal: the destruction of the world, and its immolation on the fiery altar of their dark and secret god.

"It's hard to believe, I know. But there are many others who think as I do, who are determined as I am to stop them. Apart we can accomplish little, but together we're a force to be reckoned with. Together we form an army of light set in eternal opposition to theirs of darkness.

"So far the fighting has been limited. It isn't easy to engage an enemy who refuses to show himself. We can't catch him at his work, though we can trace his activities afterward through newspaper and TV accounts of war and politics and crime. Only when he finds it necessary to employ cruder measures do we encounter him face to face, as I did tonight in those young men who attacked me.

"But one day, very soon now, his preparations will be made. The world will be poised on the edge of ruin, where the force of a single breath may suffice to push it over or hold it back. On that day they will declare themselves at last, the dogs of Hastur, the slaves of the Yellow Sign. And on that day we will open the way to our friends from above, and join with our enemies in the final battle, the Armageddon that must forever decide the fate of the earth and the disposition of its people."

Leo shifted uneasily in his chair. He had been made increasingly uncomfortable by the other's speech. By now it was clear to him that his host was either a religious fanatic or a flying saucer nut, and that it was only a matter of time before he brought out his scriptures and his tracts. Suddenly Leo was very anxious to be gone. He glanced at his watch.

"God, look at the time! It's after two already. I'd better get going or we'll neither of us get any sleep tonight."

But the threat of Leo's departure seemed to shock the old man into something closer to reality.

"I guess you think I'm pretty crazy," he said in a more natural voice. "I can't say I blame you. I'd have thought the same when *I* was in your shoes, not knowing half of what I know today. Well, it *is* late as you say. I won't try to keep you. But before you go, there's something I want to show you. I believe I saw you admiring my TV set."

"Yes," said Leo half against his will. "I don't think I've ever seen one like it. Did you build it yourself?"

"No. But I made some modifications to give it power and range. Go ahead, turn it on. It's the little black knob on the lower right."

Leo did as the old man instructed, with the same results as before.

"I don't think it's working," he said.

"It's working fine. It just needs time to warm up."

The old man was right. The humming was louder now, the picture clearer. Leo looked at it more closely, beginning to pick out images through the snow. He was looking at what appeared to be a dark plain under a dark sky. The plain was flat and empty, but it glistened here and there with what seemed to be patches of real snow. The sky was full of stars, brighter and more abundant than could be seen from anywhere on earth.

Of course, the snow on the plain and the stars in the sky might both be illusions created by poor reception. But there was no such explanation for the strange figures which Leo now saw coming into view. At first he took them for some kind of insect, for there was something definitely insectile about their armored bodies and oddly jointed limbs. But insects do not walk on their hind legs like men, nor do they use their forelegs to manipulate instruments of metal and crystal.

Yet there was nothing in this that Leo could not have seen in any number of science fiction films. The startling thing was that the creatures seemed to be as aware of him as he was of them. One by one they laid down their instruments and came to stand before him in a buzzing, chittering crowd. They had nothing that he could recognize as a face, but their attitude bespoke an intensity of interest that he found uncomfortable, even threatening. It was as if they could see him through the screen.

"What *is* this?" he asked, unable to look away.

"Not quite what you expected to see, is it?" the old man said somewhere behind him. "But you can't go poking your nose where it doesn't belong and not get caught by it sooner or later. You thought you were very clever, posing as the old man's rescuer to find out his place of refuge. But you've found out more than you bargained for.

"You might have gotten away with it if you hadn't betrayed yourself with your interest in my TV set. As you've probably guessed, this isn't a movie. Strictly speaking, it isn't even television. It allows one to see farther than television ever could, to the shores of the lake of Hali, to the black towers of Carcosa, even to the throne of the Veiled King himself. And it allows one to do more than see, as you will learn in a moment when my friends start coming through the screen."

Leo could not believe what he was hearing. This was worse than religious fanaticism. The old man was clearly insane. As if his imaginary conspiracy were not bad enough, now he had expanded his paranoid delusion, confusing his rescuer with the punks he had been rescued from. In such a state he might be dangerous. But when Leo turned to try to calm him, his soothing words died on his lips.

For the old man had changed. His face had gone gray and indistinct, as if all life and color had been drained out of it. That might have been no more than a trick of the weird light that fell upon it from the glowing screen. But he continued to change as Leo watched. His face melted, his body swelled and erupted in strange new limbs, until Leo was forced to recognize that it was no longer the old man that stood before him. It was a man-sized crab or spider, the very image of the monsters on the screen.

But to think was to be lost. For the second time that night Leo acted on pure instinct. He grabbed the lamp and threw it at the chittering horror. The lamp smashed against its banded shell, drenching it from head to foot with liquid fire. Leo fell back before the explosion of searing heat, before the unearthly writhing and howling of the tortured thing in its midst. Then he turned and ran out the door into the brightening hallway.

When Leo stumbled into the street a few minutes later, he found five young white men waiting for him, leaning with folded arms against the side of his pickup. At any other time their appearance would have been menacing, but Leo was too relieved to see his fellow humans to notice anything wrong.

"You were right . . . about the old man," he gasped. "He was a monster . . . not human. Fortunately . . . I found out in time. I killed him."

The five young men looked up as one toward the top story of the building behind him. It was already engulfed in flames. The orange light fell upon their upturned faces smooth and expressionless, their eyes black and empty as holes in a mask.

Then the eyes turned back to Leo. As at an unspoken signal the five men started toward him. At the last moment he threw up his fist to strike one of the impassive faces. It fell to the sidewalk at his feet.

# WHAT ROUGH BEAST

Mitch had not imagined the light after all. It reappeared in the darkness at the side of the road as soon as he passed its position. There it was in his rearview mirror, waving frantically from side to side in an unmistakable bid for his attention. He was so fascinated by its movement that he drove another hundred feet before he remembered to stop.

He looked back over his shoulder. The light was still there, the one bright spot in all that heavy darkness, the one outstanding feature in all those miles of rolling asphalt and grassy hills. Only now it was coming toward him. Soon it became a flashlight in the hand of a walking figure. But it was not until the figure walked into the red glow of his taillights that he saw it was a girl.

At least she did not *look* dangerous. She was very young, to begin with, probably no more than twenty. Her straight black hair, shapeless brown dress and heavy walking shoes made her look like a refugee from the sixties. She carried a heavy cloth bag hanging by a strap over one shoulder, and walked with a noticeable limp as if her feet were hurting her. But maybe she had to walk that way to carry her pregnant belly.

Mitch stuck his head out the window as she came up beside him. "Need some help?" he asked.

"How about a lift?"

"Get in."

The girl went around the front of the car and opened the door on the passenger's side. She threw her bag into the back seat and eased herself into the front. Mitch waited until she had closed the door and belted herself in before he rolled the car forward again.

"My name's Mitch," he said then. "What's yours?"

"Danny. It's short for Danielle. Thanks for stopping, Mitch. You really saved my life."

"Don't mention it. I've been driving all night with a busted radio. Having somebody to talk to will help me stay awake."

"Going far?"

"Far enough. I have to be in LA before morning."

"Is that where you're from, LA?"

"Yes."

"What are you doing way up here?"

"A guy I know offered me a job. It sounded good, so I came up to look the place over. But it wasn't any better than what I could do for myself at home. So now I'm going back again. I have to drive all night to be at my old job tomorrow morning. What about you?"

"Me? Not far. I have friends in town. I'm going to stay with them awhile."

"You're lucky I came by. Otherwise you might have had to stay out *here* all night. I can't remember the last time I saw another car on the road. Or off it either. Where did you break down?"

"I didn't break down. I was walking."

"Hitching, you mean. That's not very safe."

"Neither is picking up a hitcher."

"All I'm saying is, why take unnecessary risks? When you could just as easily get a friend to drive you."

"I don't have any friends, okay? Not here I don't. If I did, maybe I wouldn't have to leave."

Mitch looked reproachfully at the girl on the seat beside him. Her expression was unreadable in the soft light of the dash.

"I'm sorry. I shouldn't have snapped at you like that."

Mitch shrugged. "I'm only the driver."

"No, I mean it. I know you're trying to help, and I'm very grateful. It's just that I'm under a lot of stress right now."

"Apology accepted. But I'm still wondering why you had to be on your own out here. I thought these small farming communities were pretty close-knit."

"Close-knit. We're that all right. Maybe that's part of the problem."

"How do you mean?"

"You're from the city. I've never lived there myself, but I've known people who have. Things are different there. It's crowded, but it's private too. When people are cramped so close together, they *have* to ignore their neighbors to keep from driving each other crazy. But here in the country it's the dullness and loneliness that make us crazy, and the business of our neighbors that's our only relief. And if you slip up and do something stupid, we practically eat you alive."

"That sounds like the voice of experience."

Danny laid her hands on her swollen belly.

"What gave me away? I guess it *is* pretty obvious. When a girl's in her ninth month there isn't a lot she can do to hide it. I made a mistake, I know that now. But I'm trying to make up for it. I'm trying to do what's right. You'd think people would understand that and want to help me, or at least not stand in my way. You'd think my own mother and father would. But they're just as bad as everyone else. Don't get me wrong. They love me, and they've always tried to be good to me. But they're religious, you know? They haven't said it in so many words, but they see me as a miserable sinner whose sin disgraces them as much as me. Maybe I am, at that. Anyway, it seemed like the best thing I could do was to take a break from them for a while. That's why I'm going away."

Mitch nodded, partly to acknowledge Danny's story, and partly to cover his own inability to come up with a better response. He felt sorry for this girl, as he would have felt sorry for any girl who found herself in a similar situation. But there was nothing he could say or do that would make it any easier for her. He had enough troubles in his own life without taking on hers as well. He would drive her as far as she wanted to go. After that he would have to trust her to know how to take care of herself.

Presently a signboard appeared on their right. "EAT HERE GET GAS," it proclaimed in a sorry attempt at folksy humor. The signboard was weathered and faded, but the electric bulb shining down on it and the brightly lit diner behind it showed that the place was still open for business. Mitch slowed down and turned into the unpaved parking lot.

"What are you doing?" Danny asked.

"I'm going to get us something to eat."

He parked the car and got out. The girl made no move to follow him.

"Aren't you coming?"

"I'd rather wait in the car."

"Come on, Danny. It'll be my treat. You wouldn't want me to eat alone, would you?"

She looked out at the parking lot. There was not much to see there, only a couple of pickup trucks parked close under the diner window.

"Maybe a short stop won't hurt."

The diner was as empty as the parking lot, with only two other people to be seen. One was a waitress, a tired-looking woman with gray hair, standing behind the counter tending to the coffee-maker. The other was a customer, an old man in a red plaid jacket, sitting at the counter hunched over a ceramic mug. Mitch sat down in a booth by the window while Danny excused herself and disappeared into the ladies' room. The waitress came over and took his order for apple pie and coffee. She seemed to hesitate.

"Is anything wrong?" he asked.

"Your wife," she answered. "Is she okay in there? She looked about due to me."

"I'm sure she's okay. But she's not my wife. I picked her up on the road a little way back. I'm giving her a lift into town."

The waitress opened her mouth to say something else. But at that moment Danny reappeared from the ladies' room. The waitress withdrew behind the counter.

"What did she say to you?" Danny asked in a low voice as she sat down.

"Not much. She thought you looked about due, and asked if you were okay in there. Why?"

"Look."

She tipped her head across the room to where the waitress and the old man were huddled together in quiet conversation. The man glanced furtively at the young people, then got up and headed for the door.

"We have to go," Danny said then.

"Why? We haven't even had our coffee yet."

"There's no time to explain. We have to go *now.*"

Mitch tossed a couple of bills on the table and followed her out to the car. The old man was nowhere to be seen. As they pulled out onto the road he said:

"Want to tell me what happened back there?"

"Just what I was afraid would happen. They recognized me. They'll tell the others where I am."

"What others? Your parents? Why do you care? Don't they know you're going to visit your friends?"

"No. I didn't tell them."

"You didn't tell— What are you doing, running away? How old *are* you, Danny?"

"I'm legal, if that's what you're worried about. I have my driver's license here to prove it—if I can find it in the dark—"

"I'll take your word for it. Anyway, I can't look at it while I'm driving."

"And what if I *am* running away? People can have good reasons for doing that, can't they? What can you do *except* run away when people are chasing you?"

"So now people are chasing you."

"They weren't before. But now that they know where I am— God! Why did I let you talk me into going into that diner?"

"Now just a minute! Nobody forced you to go in. And how was I supposed to know you didn't want to be seen? You never told me that. You said you were just taking a break from your parents."

"I know. And I'm sorry. But I didn't lie to you, Mitch. I told you I was having trouble with my parents, and that's true. What I didn't tell you is that my parents aren't alone. You said yourself that these small farming communities are close-knit. Our community is knit a lot closer than most, and a lot more controlling of what goes on inside it. They already run my parent's lives, and now they want to run mine. That's why they'll come after me. That's why I have to run away."

"My God, Danny! You make it sound like some kind of cult."

"What if I do? There are cults in the world, aren't there, Mitch? And not all of them take on forms that are obvious to outsiders. Some of them might even look like ordinary farming communities built around ordinary country churches, the kind that preach Sunday sermons about peace and love and eternal salvation.

"That's how this one started out. But a couple of years ago it began to change. Maybe it had to change. Maybe the community would have died without it. Communities do die, you know, and this one had been failing for years. The old people who built it had mostly died themselves. The young people who grew up in it had either moved away or dropped out from lack of interest. The only ones left were people like my parents, people who didn't want or couldn't afford to leave the valley and the church they had lived in all their lives, but who didn't know how to make them thrive, either. Until Brother Angel showed them the way."

"Brother Angel? What was he, some kind of monk?"

"He was our new pastor, brought in to replace the old one when he grew too old and tired for the job. He wasn't called Brother Angel then, but he deserved the name. With him in the pulpit, the pews began to fill up again. Young people returned to the fold in ever increasing numbers. There aren't as many people living in the whole valley as we saw attending one of Brother Angel's sermons. We thought that only a miracle could move so many people at the same time to seek their salvation in our little church. But we should have realized even then that it was only Brother Angel the people came to see.

"Maybe we did notice that he wasn't as perfect as he seemed, that some of his ideas were a little strange. That didn't look so bad at first. It was such a little vice compared to his many virtues, and it was hard to fault his methods when we were so happy with the results. But what we didn't see was that his single failing had somehow become the driving force behind his overall success. His ideas were strange, but they were strange in ways that people could relate to. Take the emphasis he put on cycles and seasons, the nurturing sun and the fertile earth. Maybe that doesn't sound like much to a city dweller. But here, where everyone lives by farming and ranching, crops and herds and the things that promote them are the most important things there are. Brother Angel only gave them back the prominence that was rightfully theirs, that they had been missing for so long.

"It made it even easier to accept his ideas when our harvests started coming in in record-breaking abundance. But only the most abundant harvest could have made it easier to accept what happened then. Because then, when he was secure in his position and confident in the loyalty of his followers, he showed us how strange his ideas *really* were. He told us that the Christianity we followed is no better and no worse than any other religion. All religions and all gods have a single source and a single purpose, to reveal to us their portion of the ultimate truth. But each revelation is specific to the people who receive it, and with the passing of time it becomes forgotten, distorted, deliberately perverted by evil men. So religions and civilizations become perverted too, as we see here in our own place and time. But our hope and salvation lies in the promise of a *new* god and a *new* revelation, to come from the source of *all* gods and revelations, the womb of the Great Mother of us all.

"It sounds crazy, I know. But it sounds sane and normal compared to some of the rituals he led us in. Like sacrificing live animals in church and anointing the faithful with their blood. Or gathering unmarried girls in an empty field on a summer night, to make them get drunk on wine and dance naked around a bonfire. I held out against it as long as I could. But it isn't easy to hold yourself back when everyone around you is determined to move you forward. And it gets to be awfully lonely when going forward is made the one condition of your being treated like a human being by even your closest kin. Your only choice is to run away. So this evening, when my parents were out, I packed up my things and left."

This time Mitch did not even bother to nod. He did not know which annoyed him more, the girl for trying to feed him that garbage, or himself for almost swallowing it. He had to admit, she had really kept him going for a while. It had taken that part about the blood to show her lie for what it was. But there was no point in calling her on it. She did not have to tell him the truth. She did not have to tell him anything. As a matter of fact, he preferred it that way. The less he knew about her, the better off he would be.

But now he had something more important to think about. A pair of headlights had appeared in his rearview mirror, headlights surmounted by the flashing red dome of a police car.

"Where did *he* come from?" he muttered.

Danny turned to look out the rear window.

"Can't you outrun him?"

Mitch ignored the question. He pulled over onto the unpaved shoulder and slowed to a stop. The police car pulled up and stopped close behind them. A moment later the door opened and the officer got out and walked up to Mitch's car. Curiously, he approached on the passenger's side.

"Anything wrong, Deputy?" Mitch asked.

The officer, whom Mitch had correctly identified as a deputy sheriff, was a large man with a close-cropped head. That was as much as Mitch saw of him before the other's flashlight blinded him. By the time he could see again, the flashlight had turned back on Danny.

"Evening, Sister Danny," the deputy said.

"That's not my name. It's—"

"It won't do you no good to lie, Sister. I've been on the lookout for you. Brother Angel sent word you might be coming this way. Whatever was you thinking of, running off like that? Folks are worried sick over you, what with the Sabbath being tomorrow and all the preparation still needing to be done—"

"I don't want any part of your Sabbath. I just want to go away."

"I see you've been won over by the lies of the Enemy. Brother Angel said it might be so. He also said it won't matter for the part you have to play."

He opened the car door.

"Get out."

But Danny did not get out. She pulled away to the center of the car. So the deputy leaned in after her, caught her by the wrists and started to drag her out by force.

"No! Let go! You're hurting! *Help me, Mitch!*"

Normally Mitch would have been the last man to interfere with an officer of the law in the performance of his duty. But all this talk of Brother Angel and the Sabbath had convinced him that Danny had not lied to him, that the deputy was not an officer of the law but the agent of a lunatic pagan cult. So that when he started to drag the girl away, Mitch had no choice but to act. On the seat beside him lay Danny's flashlight. He picked it up and swung it hard at the base of the deputy's skull.

It was an awkward swing in that cramped space, but it served its purpose. The deputy grunted and fell forward across Danny's knees. She stared down at him in wide-eyed horror until Mitch came around to drag him off.

He left him lying on the shoulder under the headlights of his empty car. Then he got back into his own car with Danny and pulled back out onto the road. The headlights behind them dwindled almost to nothing before either of them spoke again.

"Is he dead?" she asked then.

"No. Just unconscious. But he should stay out long enough for us to get away."

"It doesn't matter. Others will come to take his place. The whole valley will come after us if that's what it takes to get us back. Me and my baby."

Mitch glanced at the girl in the soft light of the dash. She was looking down at her two arms folded protectively over the fullness of her belly, over the precious cargo it contained.

"Angel's baby too, though he thinks I don't know it. I know it. I've known it since that night in the field, when he came to us out of the darkness in answer to our moaning prayers. He was so beautiful. He was naked as we were, and his face was covered with a goat's-head mask. But I knew him. I knew him just the same. There must have been a hundred of us gathered there, all willing and beautiful and young. But of all of us it was only me—me, Danny Woods—that he chose. And while the others stayed by the fire and wailed their disappointment, he took my hand and led me away into the silent darkness under the trees.

"And even if I hadn't known then, I would have known later from the way the others treated me. You'd think they would have hated me for the favor he had shown to me. But no. Everyone around me was friendly and loving. Everyone was attentive to my comfort and health. Later, when I found out I was pregnant, I thought I understood why. For a child to be born to our

*"Angel's baby too, though he thinks I don't know it. I know it. I've known it since that night in the field, when he came to us out of the darkness in answer to our moaning prayers. He was so beautiful. He was naked as we were, and his face was covered with a goat's-head mask. But I knew him. I knew him just the same."*

spiritual leader was a reason for rejoicing. For a woman to be chosen to bear that child was a privilege and an honor. And I was the chosen one, the beloved one.

"But I didn't care about any of that. I only cared about Angel. And he cared about me too. At least, everyone assured me he did. But what were all their assurances worth when Angel himself stayed away from me? I couldn't fault their excuses. He was busy with the work of the Church, which was going forward now as never before. He was preparing for the coming Sabbath, the great festival on which our bountiful harvest depended. I couldn't fault their excuses. But it wasn't long before I figured out that this was all they were, excuses to cover up the fact that Angel was avoiding me.

"I waited for him as long as I could, but I couldn't wait forever. And even if I could wait, my baby could not. Finally I had to force the issue in the only way I knew how. If Angel wouldn't see me, then I wouldn't cooperate with him. I would refuse to take part in his precious rituals, though I had always taken such a central part before. The others tried to change my mind, but I wouldn't let them. I told them I had reasons for what I did, reasons I would explain only to Angel.

"And they must have believed me, because last night he came to me. But our reunion was nothing like what I had planned. He was still beautiful. I almost forgot how angry I was when I saw him. Yet he spoke to me so sternly. How dare I let my petty concerns interfere with the great work required of me? How dare I withhold myself from the rituals? Did I still not know how important they were? Even now the cycle of life was returning to the starting place, and the womb of the Great Mother was swelling to the full. Soon the cycle would be complete, and the womb would expel into the world the new god we waited for. The god whose coming would signal the start of the cleansing time, when the world would shake off its plaguing cities as a great beast shakes off stinging flies. The god whose power would remake the world for the greater glory of the Great Mother of us all. For the greater glory of Shub-Niggurath, the Black Goat of the Woods with a Thousand Young!

"That was how he talked. I couldn't follow all of it. But I could follow enough to understand how different we were in our desires. I wanted my lover and the father of my baby. He wanted only his god. But I wanted to stay with him even then. I would have done it except for one thing. He told me that my baby and I still had an important part to play in his great work, maybe the most important part of all. He didn't say what part it was, but to me it was obvious. My baby was to be murdered, sacrificed in some horrible rite to hurry the coming of his god."

The girl was silent now. Mitch looked again in her direction. Her position had changed little, yet she seemed to have collapsed into a tight ball of woe.

"I believe you," he said then, because he had to say something. "It's no crazier than some other things that are going on these days. The news is full of crazy cults. There seem to be more of them all the time now that the millennium is coming to an end. If those are real, then there's no reason that this can't be real also. And that's too bad, because it means we have more than just the law to deal with."

He glanced at the rearview mirror.

"We're being followed. We have been for some time, almost since we left the deputy. Maybe it's the deputy himself, recovered in time to come after us. Or maybe he has a friend. But why is he staying back so far? That's just asking us to make a break for it, unless—"

But Mitch did not finish his sentence. Ahead of them was something that finished it far more effectively than he ever could. The road there was bounded by two black wedges of opposing hills. Two pickup trucks were parked across it end to end, and a crowd of people with lanterns and guns was standing in front of them.

"What are we slowing down for?" Danny demanded. "Drive through them!"

"I *can't* drive through them!"

"Then turn around!"

"What if they shoot?"

"They won't shoot. They won't risk hitting the baby."

It sounded reasonable. But as he turned and sped away he heard the sound of a shot, followed by the louder sound of a tire blowing out. He slammed on the brake, but the car had other ideas. It swerved off the road across the right shoulder and dropped its nose into the ditch beyond.

Danny was the first to recover. "*Run, Mitch, run!*" she yelled. Then she jumped out of the car and bounded across the lighted ditch toward the dark slope on the other side. Mitch paused long enough to find her flashlight, then jumped out after her.

At first they ran in the headlight beams, but after they crossed the first rise they ran in blind darkness. Mitch did not like to use the flashlight for fear of giving away their position. But there was no way they could *not* give away their position, with the deep swath their legs were cutting in the waist-high grass. And there was no way he could follow her without it. It was wonderful how quickly she covered the ground. He would not have believed that anyone as pregnant as she was could move like that. But he might have known she could not keep it up forever. She caught her foot in the heavy grass and fell forward on her face.

She rolled over onto her back as Mitch came up and knelt beside her.

"Are you hurt?" he asked breathlessly. "Can you stand up?"

"It isn't that. I think—I think I'm in—" She clutched his arm like a drowning woman. "Oh, Mitch, I'm sorry. Sorry for dragging you into this.

Sorry for everything."

Mitch looked back the way they had come. All the dark rise was between them and the road, but the thunder of engines and the false dawn of headlights left no doubt what was happening there. He turned to the girl again.

"It's not your fault," he said then. "But now I need you to listen. You can't keep going in the shape you're in, and they'll catch us if we stop. But I have a plan. I'll go back and try to lead them away from you. You stay here until you hear us go past, then get back down to the road. I'll circle around and join you there. With any luck, we'll drive out of here in one of their cars. Okay?"

"Okay, Mitch. But try not to be too long. I'm scared."

He patted her hand to comfort her, then gently but firmly pulled himself away.

Alone, he followed the lights and noises to the top of the rise. He approached the crest on his hands and knees and raised his head above the tall grass to look down at the road below. It was worse than he had expected. There must be half a dozen cars and trucks down there, with maybe two dozen people pouring out and gathering in the headlights. He even thought he recognized one or two of them. The one in the red plaid jacket might be the old man from the diner. The other in the dark suit, the fair-haired man directing things, was almost certainly Brother Angel. Mitch looked hard at this second figure, curious to see the face of the man responsible for all the excitement. But it was too far for him to see clearly. When he saw them fan out and start up the slope, he rose to his feet and prepared to put his own plan into action. But at that moment his attention was diverted by the sound of Danny's terrified scream.

It took him only a moment to get back to her. But he was already too late to save her. She lay on her back in a circle of tall grass, motionless and very pale in the spot of the flashlight beam. It was odd how calm she looked, as if all the fear and pain of her final moments had had no lasting effect on her. Because he himself would never forget seeing what those monsters had done to her. But how could they have gotten to her? And how could they have done what they did yet left no sign of their presence? The grass was not trampled or the blood tracked around the way it would have been if—

His thought was interrupted by a rustling noise from the curtain of grass behind her. Raising the flashlight beam, he saw that the curtain had opened and that a tiny face was looking out at him. It was as small as any infant's face, and as delicate in its proportions, and there was still enough blood on its waxen skin to show where it had come from. But there was nothing infant-like about those great dark eyes, preternaturally old and wise. There was nothing infant-like about that cruel smile, unmoved by the spectacle of human pain and death.

The curtain opened wider. If Mitch had still been capable of rational thought, he might have observed that Danny had been mistaken about the paternity of her child and the cultists' intentions toward it. As it was, he could only throw down his flashlight and fall forward on his face. He could only pray that those shaggy legs and cloven hooves would pass lightly over him when the new god stepped out to greet its worshippers.

# THE NEST

I'm not crazy, Doctor Eliot, in spite of what the Captain thinks. No, he didn't say it to my face. But why else would he order me to report to you for this psychiatric evaluation? Me, a decorated officer with twelve years on the force! But I don't blame him for not believing me. I guess I always knew nobody would. I guess that's why I kept quiet about it for so long, even to Clark, even to the partner who lived through most of it with me. I'd be quiet about it still if it wasn't for that news item I saw yesterday morning. The one about the Ghoul murders starting up again.

Now you want me to tell you the same story I told the Captain. I don't expect you to believe it any more than he did. But I have to tell it anyway, even if it means being kicked off the force and branded as a mental case for the rest of my life. It would be so much easier to retract my statement, to turn in my badge and walk away. But I can't do that. I have to stay and take the chance that someone will believe my story, believe it and act on it before it's too late.

It happened three months ago. You can get the exact date from our report. The Ghoul was all over the news back then, with something like eight murders to his credit. The Skid Row Ghoul. Leave it to the press to give a serial killer a colorful handle. But this one almost fit. He didn't steal corpses out of graveyards, but he preyed on the bums and winos down on Skid Row which is the next best thing. And as for eating his victims, well, I never heard a better explanation for his mutilating their bodies the way he did. But I wasn't thinking about the Ghoul riding patrol that night, and I don't suppose Clark was either. Not till we spotted Little Red Riding Hood.

That's what Clark called him when he pointed him out to me. "Look at Little Red Riding Hood!" he said, and it wasn't a bad description. The guy was wearing a slick red raincoat with a pointed hood attached. It was so obviously a woman's coat that I would have thought he was a woman except for the man's shabby boots and trousers underneath. And except that it looked so small on him. He was a couple of inches over six feet, though his funny crouching walk did a lot to hide the fact. He also had a basket of goodies, in the form of a black plastic trash bag he carried over one shoulder.

We both thought about the Ghoul then. This was exactly the sort of victim he liked, and only a couple of blocks from his usual hunting ground. So we thought it would be a good idea to give the guy a word of friendly warning. Clark pulled the car up alongside of him and I called to him out the window. And he froze. He didn't come up to the car. He didn't turn to look at me. He just stopped dead in his tracks.

We didn't think anything about that. A lot of these street people are borderline crazy anyway, and all of them are afraid of the cops. But we weren't about to back off just because the guy was a little uncomfortable. After all, we were trying to do him a favor. So I got out of the car and went up to him. I planted myself right in front of him to be sure I had his undivided attention. But he still didn't look at me. He just stood there under the lamppost with his head hanging down, his face hidden in the deep shadow of his hood.

I didn't like not being able to see who I was talking to, so I told him to take off the hood. When he didn't do it I reached over to do it for him. He did look at me then! He raised his head and looked me straight in the eyes, and I jumped back from the shock of it. But Jesus, who wouldn't jump back from a face like that, with big red eyes and yellow teeth in a wrinkled gray snout like a hairless rat or dog? It was like Little Red Riding Hood had changed into the Big Bad Wolf right before my eyes! And before I could recover he swung his bag into my chest like a baseball bat and took off running down the street.

I would have taken off after him except for one thing. The bag wasn't heavy enough or hard enough to do me any real damage. But after it hit me it fell on the sidewalk, which split it open like a rotten fruit and spilled out half its contents. And the sight of those contents stopped me as completely as if I'd been hit with a bag of bricks. Most of it wasn't the kind of stuff a guy like me with no medical training could recognize. But right on top of everything else was a human arm and hand!

It stopped Clark too when he came running up to help me. "Good Lord!" I heard him say close beside me. But the sound of his voice was all it took to snap me back into action. "It's the Ghoul!" I yelled. "Get him!"

Well, we both took off after him then. But his trick with the bag had given him a sizable lead, and he was making the most of it. He was fast on his feet in spite of his funny crouch. He ran very low to the ground, almost on all fours. At least, that's how it looked to me from half a block behind him. When I saw that we had no hope of running him down I drew my gun and yelled, "Stop or I'll shoot!" He didn't stop, and I did shoot. I took aim and fired a single shot at his back. But the shot must have missed him for all the effect it had, and I didn't have time to fire another. At the end of the block was a row of tall wooden houses. He ran up the steps of one of these and in through the open front door.

We slowed down a little when we reached the door ourselves, but there was never any question of our not going in after him. We had neither of us gotten a good look at him. There was no description we could give of him that he couldn't make useless just by ditching his raincoat and scary Halloween mask. We couldn't let him out of our sight for long without running the risk of losing him forever. Okay, maybe there were personal considerations too. If this was the guy we thought he was, then this was an important collar, maybe the most important one in years. And it had been dropped in our laps like a Christmas present. We would have been crazy to let it get away.

But there was still a chance it would get away in spite of us. You don't follow a mountain lion into a cave without putting yourself at risk, and the situation here was about the same. The killer was as dangerous as a mountain lion. There was no question that he was armed. At the very least he had the big butcher knife he used on his victims, and there was no telling what he might be carrying besides. And the house was dark and empty like a cave. It was part of a tract that was slated for demolition. The power was shut off, and the windows were boarded up to keep out squatters. And what were the odds that the mountain lion had picked this cave at random? He had known about the front door being open, so he must know something about the house behind it. He could probably find his way around it in the dark better than Clark and I could with our flashlights.

But there was one thing working in our favor. "Look!" Clark said. He pointed with his flashlight to the middle of the living room, where a trail of fresh blood drops ran away from us across the bare wooden floor. It was the killer's blood, it had to be. So my bullet hadn't missed him after all. And now Clark and I wouldn't miss him either. Because the trail showed exactly which way he had gone, and that he wouldn't have much fight in him when we found him at the end of it.

The bloody trail ran from the living room to the dining room and across the dining room to the kitchen. It looked like the only place left for it to go was outside by the back door. But there was another door in the kitchen, a closed door, and the trail ran up to and under it. This was almost too easy. We were ready to hunt the killer over the whole house, and here he was holed up in a kitchen closet. But that was no reason to let our guard down. While Clark stood on one side with his gun at the ready, I stood on the other side and yelled, "Police! Come out with your hands up!" Then I reached over, turned the knob and swung the door wide open. But the killer wasn't behind it, at least not where we could see. Because the door hadn't opened on a closet. It had opened on an enclosed staircase leading down to the basement.

That's when the smell hit us. We had noticed it before of course, almost from the moment we stepped through the front door. A rotten smell, like something had died under the floorboards. But it hadn't been bad enough to be more than a minor annoyance. It was excruciating now. Imagine a garbage bin full of spoiled meat rotting in the summer sun, and you'll have a good idea of what it was like. It was a wonder it hadn't stopped the killer from going down there. It almost stopped Clark and me. There was no way to hold our guns, our flashlights and our noses at the same time, and there was no way we were going after him without holding all three. But then Clark got an idea.

"Breathe through your mouth," he told me. I did, and the smell became almost bearable.

It was harder to deal with what we found in the basement. It wasn't the killer, not yet anyway. The trail showed that he had gone on ahead through an open door at the back. But the basement wasn't empty like the rest of the house. It was furnished with a number of old wooden produce crates lined up along one wall. And the crates weren't empty either. God! It had been bad enough when the smell was just a smell. It was horrible now that we knew what was making it. It was the missing parts of all the killer's victims! It was the killer's bag all over again, but multiplied by maybe a dozen times! What were they doing here? Had the butcher carved up all those people just to let them rot? I hoped it was just to let them rot. But some of the crates held nothing but bones, and the ends of some of the larger ones were looking kind of chewed.

I don't know what we would have done if there had been time for this last detail to sink in. But there wasn't time, because suddenly the killer was in the room with us. One moment the door at the back was just an empty frame. The next moment he was coming through it, screaming an unearthly scream and swinging a big red fire ax high over his head! But we were ready for him. We didn't give him any warning then. We just let go at him with everything we had. We emptied our guns into him as fast as we could pull the triggers. Of course it stopped him dead. He went over backward like a felled tree. The ax flew out of his hands and went clattering into a corner.

It took us a while to recover after that. But when we did, and the killer didn't show any sign of getting up again, we went up close and examined him under our flashlights. We didn't expect to find him alive after all the lead we had pumped into him. He was alive, but he wouldn't be much longer. His chest still rose and fell, but raggedly and with an awful gurgling sound deep in his throat. We would have preferred to let Nature take its course, maybe even to help it along with another bullet or two. But as long as he was still alive we had to try to keep him that way. So while I held my light steady over him, Clark got down on his knees beside him and started opening what was left of his raincoat.

The back of Clark's head kept me from seeing what he was doing, which wasn't all that interesting anyway. So I turned my attention to the face of the dying man. Jesus! I'd only gotten a taste of it in the street, but I got the full course now. It had been ugly then. But now, with the red eyes rolling up in their sockets, the jaw hanging open and the pale tongue falling out over the yellow teeth, it was worse than ugly. It made it hard to remember that the thing was just a mask. Well, I must have let the light drift because suddenly I heard Clark say, "Hold it steady, can't you?" I quickly pulled it back again. But at the same moment Clark turned away from the dying man, fell over onto his hands and knees and made a retching sound. And when I saw what he had seen I felt like retching myself.

Christ! The face was nothing compared to this. Clark had finished opening the raincoat, and the body under it was naked to the waist. It had been damaged by our bullets, but not enough to hide the fact that it looked like nothing human. It was thinly covered with blood-soaked fur, and it had eight nipples, eight of them, running in two parallel rows down the length of the chest and belly. But the thing of it was, it was real! The body, the face, the whole horrible creature was real! And the most horrible thing about it was, it had been female all along! I don't think either of us could have touched it after that. But of course by then its breathing had stopped, so there wasn't any point.

Clark was looking pretty bad, so I sent him to the car to radio for help while I stayed with the body. And that was all he knew about it. Because when he came back to the house he met me coming out, hacking and wheezing, with a big cloud of thick black smoke billowing behind me. He asked me what had happened, and I told him the monster had set fire to the house before attacking us. He wanted us to go in after the body, but I told him the house was already too involved. So we went to the car to call the fire department, and then we went back to the house and watched it burn.

That was all he knew about it, and all that got into our report. But what he didn't know, what never got into our report, was what happened in the house while I was alone.

For a while nothing did. I just stood there over the dead monster, examining it under my flashlight. This probably wasn't the best thing for my nerves, which really weren't in much better shape than Clark's. But I would rather see the monster than not see it, and I had an idea I could get used to it. After all, most of its horror had come from it being sprung on us unexpectedly. Now that it was dead and I could take my time about looking it over, it was still horrible, but it was fascinating too. What could make a human being look like that? An accident? A freak of nature? The effect of some disfiguring disease? Whatever had done it, it was a real monster now. You only had to look at the crates to see that.

Those crates. Maybe I could get used to the monster, but I could never get used to those crates. They made it pretty obvious that this so-called Ghoul had really lived up to its reputation. Okay, maybe it wasn't a real ghoul. Maybe it didn't sneak into cemeteries to rob graves and feed on corpses. But even a real ghoul would find that hard to do in a city like this one, where corpses are routinely poisoned with embalming fluid, locked in airtight metal caskets and buried in concrete vaults. Our Ghoul had gotten around all that, by making its own corpses out of people in the street, taking as much of their bodies as it could carry away and bringing them here to its underground lair to age them

*Our Ghoul had gotten around all that, by making its own corpses out of people in the street, taking as much of their bodies as it could carry away and bringing them here to its underground lair to age them in makeshift coffins. You had to admire its ingenuity. Its industry too. There must have been a lot more murders than ever got reported.*

in makeshift coffins. You had to admire its ingenuity. Its industry too. There must have been a lot more murders than ever got reported.

Suddenly I heard a noise. It wasn't a loud noise, just a kind of muffled squealing in the dark at the back of the basement. But even the softest noise can be startling if you're not expecting it, and I wasn't expecting this one. At least it didn't take me long to figure out what was making it. You couldn't leave all that food lying around without attracting something to eat it. The place must be crawling with rats. But I didn't see any rats when I swept my flashlight along the back wall. And the noise didn't stop the way rats would if you surprised them.

God, I wished Clark would hurry back. The last thing I wanted was to investigate that noise alone, and it was starting to look like I would have to. It wasn't coming from this room at all. It was coming from the room on the other side of the wall, the same room the monster had come out of to attack Clark and me. And it didn't sound like rats anymore. It sounded like someone crying through a gag. What if the monster hadn't limited itself to murdering bums and winos? What if it had kidnapped a child and kept it tied up in there? I couldn't leave it crying in the dark. Clark or no Clark, I had to take a look.

At least I didn't have to look far. The new room was half the size of the old one, and there was nothing inside it to block my view of it. I could stand in the open doorway and let my flashlight explore it for me. There were no crates in there. But there was a big pile of straw and rags in a corner at the back, a pile arranged in a sort of oversized nest. The crying noise was coming from inside the nest. But if there was anything else in there, I couldn't see it yet. Not till I walked right up to it and shone my flashlight into it.

Christ! Of all the shocks in that shock-filled night, that one was the worst. Until that moment I could still believe the Ghoul was human. Deformed, yes. Demented, yes. But at bottom as human as you and me. I could believe that real ghouls didn't exist. That even if they did exist, they couldn't survive in a world of embalmed bodies and metal caskets. But all that changed when I saw what was in the nest. Now I know that ghouls are real. That far from being starved out of our modern cities, they've been settling in like the rats and pigeons before them. That like the rats, they'll soon loose such a plague of horror as will turn our world into a little corner of hell.

Those creatures. I couldn't make out how many there were, they were so balled up together. But there were at least half a dozen and probably more. One day, if they lived, they would all be hulking dog-faced monsters with a murderous appetite for human flesh and blood. Now they were only puppies. Blind, hairless puppies huddling in the dark, crying for the mother who would never come again.

You don't believe me either, Doctor. I can see it in your face. But maybe it doesn't really matter whether you believe me or not. After all, the ghouls are still out there. This new series of killings shows that. Sooner or later one of them is bound to slip up and get caught. And maybe whoever catches it won't make the same mistake I did.

God, I hope not. Otherwise the guilt would be more than a man can bear. In that house and under it was the absolute proof of the horror I've been trying to warn you about. The proof that would have mobilized people into doing something to stop it before it's too late. The proof that would have made me a hero instead of a crazy man. And I'm the one who burned it down!

# FROM INNER EGYPT

The mummy lay under electric lights on a shiny metal table. Its unwrapped body had an unfinished look, as if a sculptor had set out to make a man of sticks and mud and given up halfway through. Only the head seemed near complete, and it looked more like an African tribal mask than anything human. The mouth was a narrow oval framing a row of white and slightly protruding teeth. The eyes were smaller ovals framing nothing. The nose and ears were pressed flat against the skull. The face, drawn tight over prominent bones, was empty of lines and wrinkles, empty of any expression but calm indifference. I have slept three thousand years, it seemed to say. Whole civilizations have risen and fallen and risen again without troubling my dreams. Then why should I wake to express surprise at anything *your* civilization may show me?

"You know, Paul, I've been with the museum two years now, but this is my first mummy. What are these shots supposed to tell you?"

Paul O'Neil looked up from the mummy to the man standing over it, the white-coated technician adjusting the X-ray apparatus with cool efficiency.

"Any number of things," he answered. "They might give us important clues about the life this fellow led, clues we couldn't get otherwise without taking him apart. Clues about the food he ate, the injuries he survived, the diseases that might have killed him."

"I get it. From his stomach and heart you can see what his diet and health were like."

"Not exactly. These mummies have no stomachs and hearts. Or brains either. The embalmers removed those organs as part of the embalming process. Their bodies are hollow, or rather they're stuffed like Thanksgiving turkeys with dried flowers and herbs. Still, we can learn a lot from what's left. Take the teeth, for instance. Most mummies have terrible teeth, worn and broken. This suggests that the bread they ate in life had a high concentration of pulverized grinding stone."

"Amazing. It sounds like you can find out everything there is to know about this guy except maybe who he is."

Paul looked again at the skeletal form with the calm, expressionless face. But I *do* know who he is, he thought. This is the guy who's going to help me add a whole new chapter to the history of ancient Egypt.

## 2

Paul had entertained no such ambition only a week before. When he began the task of unpacking and cataloging the newly arrived Carter collection, he would have been happy just to know that his work was not a complete waste of time. It was not every day that a wealthy amateur of Egyptian archeology died and left the museum his private collection. But private collections of Egyptian artifacts were not exactly common, and the better ones were generally known. The fact that nobody at the museum had ever heard of the Carter collection said little in its favor.

That was what Paul thought going in. And the first few pieces he examined did nothing to change his opinion. The collection seemed to be chiefly remarkable for the way it mixed genuine antiquities with obvious fakes, suggesting that the collector himself had been none too clear about the difference. But even the genuine antiquities were heavily weighted toward third-rate examples of objects that had already been seen and described many times before.

Then Paul came to the unwrapped mummy and its accompanying scroll. At first he did not know what to make of them. Carter himself seemed to have regarded them as the twin jewels of his collection, but at first glance it was difficult to see why. Neither was remarkable in appearance. The mummy was not even particularly well preserved. The scroll was a simple papyrus roll inscribed with little art, as if the scribe had had no concern except to get his record down. But the record itself was an historical account, a kind of memorial to the man it was buried with. It was this account that finally awakened Paul's interest.

According to the scroll, the mummy was that of a great magician who had exercised a pervasive influence over the Egypt of his day, a thousand years before the start of the Christian era. His story was fantastic enough for three magicians. He was not even heard of until the day he walked out of the empty desert to present himself at the pharaoh's court. But there he demonstrated such godlike powers that the pharaoh declared him a god in human form and submitted himself to his teachings. Under the magician's direction, the pharaoh decreed that the old gods of Egypt had been deposed by new gods who were older than Egypt, and that the worship of these new gods would be enforced among the people. As for the priests of the deposed gods, they could either transfer their allegiance to the new gods and live, or die as sacrifices on their rededicated altars.

The priests were outraged by this turn of events. But they were not prepared to stand up against the combined might of the pharaoh's armies and the magician's powers. They had no choice but to accept life under the terms that were offered them. But in their hearts they remained true to the old gods, and they encouraged their people to do likewise. In public they led their people in the lesser rites of the new gods, and in preparations for the greater rites to come. In private they cursed the upstart gods and plotted against the men who spoke for them. And when the time came for the priests to take part in the magician's ultimate rite, a terrific holocaust of fire and blood meant to purify the world for the return of the gods themselves, it was their own plan they put into action.

Their rebellion was sudden and complete. They drove the pharaoh from his palace, hunted him across the desert and ultimately killed him. They also killed the few traitor priests before the temples of the gods they had betrayed. But the magician they did not kill. He too fled into the desert, accompanied by a handful of his most loyal followers. And there, after instructing those by him to expect his swift return, he died and was secretly buried.

"It's a remarkable story on several counts. But the most remarkable thing about it is the names of the people involved. The pharaoh's name is Nephren-Ka. And the magician who caused all the trouble, the magician whose mummy was unearthed with the scroll and is now stored with it in the museum basement, *his* name is Nyarlathotep."

Paul was outlining his discovery to Dr. Howard, the department head, as the two men sat across the desk from each other in Howard's office. Ending his speech on this dramatic note, he leaned back in his chair and prepared to enjoy the response it clearly deserved. He was surprised and disappointed when it was met with frowning silence.

"Maybe you don't know about Nyarlathotep?" he asked.

"Yes," Howard answered, "I know about Nyarlathotep. I know about the great Egyptian prophet of the pre-Egyptian gods. And I know about Nephren-Ka, the pharaoh who introduced his reluctant people to the worship of those gods. But more importantly, I know that none of them, not the heretical prophet, the pharaoh he seduced or the monstrous gods they both adored, have any existence outside the worthless pages of ancient occultists like Alhazred and Prinn."

Paul stood his ground, or tried to.

"I assure you, Dr. Howard, I put no trust in occultists, ancient or otherwise. Prinn was a notorious charlatan even in his own day, and if Alhazred believed a fraction of what he put in his book, he deserved to be called mad. But even charlatans and madmen may tell the truth on occasion, and when their statements receive outside confirmation they ought to be investigated. If you'll just consider the evidence—"

"What evidence? The scroll? We know nothing of its origin. We can trace its history back only as far as its inclusion in the Carter collection, a collection which, as you yourself admit, is already rife with forgeries. The mummy? An unwrapped mummy is as difficult to trace as any other dead man found without clothes or distinguishing marks. And to top it off, the scroll may not even belong to him. For all we know, the scroll and the mummy were first brought together by an unscrupulous dealer to drive up the price of both."

Now it was Paul's turn to be silent. But something in his face must have shown what he was feeling, because when Howard spoke again it was in a softer tone.

"I'm sorry, Paul. I realize how disappointed you must be. We've all had the same dream at one time or another, the dream of finding something big. It isn't a bad dream. Our knowledge could never have advanced as far as it has without it. But if we allow the dream to lead us away from sound scientific principles, which way would our knowledge go then? No, my boy, it's good to be a dreamer. But be a scientist first."

3

Returning to his own office a short time later, Paul unlocked the door to let himself in. He kept his office locked all the time now, like everyone else since the start of the current crime wave. Maybe crime wave was too strong a term for a string of thefts too inconsequential to amount to more than pranks. But what they lacked in weight they made up for in number, with three of them falling in the space of a single week. Besides, they did not feel like pranks when you were one of the victims. His own office was the first one hit, his entire collection of hieroglyphic lexicons wiped out overnight. True, they were none of them particularly rare or valuable books. But it would take time to replace them, time like now when he needed them most.

His interview with the department head could not have gone worse. Maybe it was to be expected that a discovery like his would be met with a certain amount of scientific skepticism, but Howard's response had taken this beyond all reasonable bounds. What was behind his hostile attitude? It could not be the weakness of Paul's evidence that he objected to, since he had not even given Paul a chance to present it. But if it was not the evidence in support of Paul's theory, then maybe it was the theory itself. After all, Nyarlathotep and Nephren-Ka had been the exclusive province of the occultists for the last three thousand years. Their sudden intrusion into the domain of serious archeology could only be taken by a scientist like Howard as an obscene and blasphemous joke.

But whatever the grounds for Howard's objections, it was not they that would keep Paul from getting a serious hearing for his find. It was the fact that they were almost certain to be shared by everyone else in the field. Which meant that there was little hope for Paul to circumvent him. If Paul was to gain the acceptance of the scientific community, he must present a case compelling enough to convince Howard himself.

Sitting at his desk, Paul unlocked and opened the shallow top drawer, took out a thin stack of manila folders and laid them before him on the desktop. All his evidence was here in these three folders, all the data he had been able to find relating to Nyarlathotep and the Carter mummy. He had gathered it in a single week, working at night or during odd hours stolen from the performance of his regular duties. There must be enough material here to prove his theory many times over. It only needed to be sorted and arranged to show to its best advantage.

He pulled down the first folder and started turning through its contents. This was a complete facsimile of the Carter scroll, presented section by section in a series of numbered photographs. The original was locked in the museum basement, but its color and texture were well represented by these photographic plates. The physical scroll was the best argument for its own authenticity. Few forgers would have possessed the skill to create such a thing, and fewer still would have possessed the knowledge, at least until comparatively recent times. And the scroll was obviously old. Moreover, its age could be verified with scientific tests. But it was not the scroll whose authenticity he wanted to prove, so much as the history it contained. Without more substantial corroboration it was only an interesting fairy tale.

He pulled down the second folder. This contained his translation of the scroll, penciled in longhand on a dozen loose sheets of ruled yellow paper. The story it told was in all its essentials the one he had outlined for Howard earlier. Its telling was crude by anyone's standards, as he had noted at the time. But its very crudeness gave it an air of truthful simplicity that a more artful presentation might have lacked. Still, a creditable history needed more than that. At the very least it needed to be consistent with the culture that had produced it, and it would be hard to imagine a history less consistent than the one presented here. It was bad enough that it took for its subject two men whose names had all but disappeared from the annals of their people, and ascribed to them a set of deeds that should have fixed them there forever. But it also contradicted their people's most basic beliefs about death and resurrection. The ancient Egyptians would not have rejected the notion of Nyarlathotep's return. But they would have looked for it in a dim and mystical future, not within the lifetime of those who had buried him.

Maybe the scroll's inconsistencies would appear less damning if they could be harmonized with other sources of suitable age and authority. The third folder contained a collection of such sources, citations and excerpts from all the references to Nyarlathotep and Nephren-Ka that Paul had been able to find. But most of them were unfortunately derived from the discredited writings of Alhazred and Prinn. And even they were less helpful than they might have been. These on Nephren-Ka all told the same story, of a pharaoh whose excesses caused him to be driven from his throne and hunted to his death by his own subjects. But these on Nyarlathotep were all very different. Here he was a god of Egyptian magic, a shadowy figure whose terrific power could still be tapped by black magicians who conjured in his name. Here he was an inverted spiritual leader, the evil Christ or Moses who would one day drag the world back down to the chaotic hell from which it had risen at the dawn of time. Here he was a personification of the primal chaos itself, a ravening monster demanding sacrifices of human flesh and blood.

Paul pushed the third folder away and buried his face in his hands. Was this what his evidence amounted to? A scroll whose origin could not be proved, a translation no better than the document it was made from, and a collection of unrelated notes that added nothing to either? What had possessed him to believe he could convince old Howard with these? Maybe Howard was right after all, and he had let his desire for an important find impair his better judgment. He only hoped this realization had not come too late for him to undo some of the damage he had done to himself in Howard's eyes.

4

"Paul!"

He looked up from his desk to see a colleague looking back at him from the open doorway.

"Howard wants to see you right away. He's downstairs in the basement storeroom."

"Wants to see me? What about?"

But the other was already gone.

Paul had never thought he would welcome the call to one of Howard's meetings. But he had reached the stage where he would have welcomed anything that would put an end to his endless investigation. He had given half the day to his search, and here he was at the end of it no farther along than when he began. His only regret was that his colleague had gone before Paul could ask him what the meeting was about. But he would find out soon enough. The basement storeroom was already in front of him.

It was something big, whatever else it was. The whole department was here ahead of him. The door was so crowded with white-coated backs that it was hard for Paul to squeeze himself in, and even harder to find a place where he could see what the others were looking at. But when he *could* see he was no more enlightened than before. What was this to command their interest? It was only a large work table. It was only a collection of books and artifacts arranged in a careless semicircle in front of the single chair.

Dr. Howard was standing before the table, with his back to the door. He turned as Paul came in.

"Ah, Paul, there you are. Come up here, please, and have a look at these."

The wall of backs opened to let Paul pass through and join Howard at the table. But even there the reason for their interest was a mystery. Though the collection of books was certainly a strange one. Egyptian themes predominated, but the subjects ranged far beyond these, from mathematics and history to astronomy and physics. And the levels varied just as wildly. Paul saw a child's hieroglyphic dictionary standing side by side with a scholar's lexicon. But it was not until he recognized the latter volume as one that had disappeared from his own office the week before, that he realized what this collection was.

"Are these your books?" Howard asked.

"Yes, some of them. But these others—"

"I know. Our burglar must be branching out, hitting other departments than ours. The gift shop, too, by the look of it. It's perfectly scandalous, the way he makes himself free of the place. But the *real* scandal is the way the head office refuses to take it seriously. After all, they tell me, nothing important has been stolen, nothing whose loss would outweigh the bad publicity we'd receive if the real police were called in. The fools! Don't they understand that if they give this fellow the run of the museum, it's only a matter of time before he steals something important enough to force their hands? Maybe *this* will convince them. But it makes no sense! Why take the trouble to steal these things, only to leave them here? And why these things in particular? A magpie could come up with a more coherent collection."

Why indeed? Paul wondered. The books were every bit as senseless as Howard said they were. And the artifacts were no better. An antique oil lamp and a modern reproduction Rosetta stone, why had the burglar collected these? Maybe the oil lamp was valuable in itself, but the Rosetta stone was only a cheap imitation. Still, it was an imitation of the single most important artifact in the whole field of Egyptian studies, the stone whose parallel Greek and Egyptian inscriptions had unlocked the secrets of the Egyptian hieroglyphs. Could it unlock the burglar's secrets as well? Had he gathered these materials to help him read the ancient writings? But if that was so, then where were the ancient writings he was preparing to read? The remaining books were all in modern English. Unless—

"We won't waste our time looking for motives," Howard said. "The man's a lunatic. He doesn't need more motive than that. Roger, I think we've seen all we're going to see. Arrange to have these things cleared away. The rest of you—"

"Excuse me, Dr. Howard. Wouldn't it be better to leave the room as it is?"

"Good thinking, Paul. There may be something here that the police can use to catch the burglar. Never mind, Roger. The rest of you, get back to work."

But Paul was not thinking about the police. What he was thinking he would not admit even to himself. Such things did not happen in a sane world, and to imagine otherwise, even for a moment, was to risk becoming a worse madman than Howard's burglar, a worse madman even than Alhazred or Prinn. And yet, try as he might, he could not dismiss the thought that the evidence before him was of something far more important than a rash of common burglaries, that it was the very evidence he was searching for himself. But there was only one way to know for sure. If he was wrong, he would have done no harm. He would even have assisted in a criminal investigation. But if he was right! He would have found such proof as would shake even Howard out of his hidebound complacency, and write his own name for all time in the history of science.

## 5

"It was the arrangement of the books that gave me the idea," Paul told Howard early the next day in the latter's office. "That made me think our burglar was using the storeroom for more than just a place to hide his loot. That he was using it for— But here, let me show you."

"Please do," Howard said.

Paul set the VCR to play. The TV screen jittered a little and then went dark.

"This is the storeroom we're looking at," he said. "I set up the camcorder last night after everyone else went home. The picture isn't very good, because an oil lamp isn't much of a light source. But we can't see anything while the room is dark. I'll just fast-forward a little."

He pressed a button and the dark screen jittered into life. After a minute or two it suddenly brightened to show a recognizable image. He pressed another button and the VCR settled back to play.

"Look!" he said triumphantly. "There he is!"

Together the two men looked at the screen, at the image of a third man sitting at a table across from them. He was bald and thin and apparently naked. His movements were stiff and slow as he turned over the pages of a book.

"What's he doing?" Howard asked.

"Studying."

"How long does he go on like that?"

"I fast-forwarded through the whole thing this morning before you came in. He goes on just as we see him for about four hours. Then the tape runs out."

"Good work, Paul! You've turned out to be quite a detective. We'll just run this tape over to security and—"

"Just a minute. Don't you notice anything strange about that figure?"

"Strange? I don't know. He looks like an escapee from a geriatric hospital. You'd think they would keep a closer eye on their patients—"

"I don't mean that. Doesn't he look, well, familiar?"

"I'm afraid you've lost me, Paul. Why should the burglar look familiar?"

"The burglar? Very well, let's talk about the burglar. His first burglary occurred six nights ago, two nights after the arrival of the Carter collection. It took place in my own office, here in the Egyptian wing, and books on Egyptian writing were stolen. Subsequent burglaries extended his range as far as the museum gift shop, collecting books on more general scientific topics along the way. But he never got far from the Egyptian wing. Yesterday we discovered that he has been making our basement storeroom his center of operations. And today we see that he has been using it as his personal library and study.

"What we don't see is, why? Why has he taken all this trouble, exposed himself to all this risk, to steal these books, these artifacts? Why has he increased his exposure by studying these things here instead of taking them away with him? And, as you yourself asked, why these things in particular? Books on anthropology, geology, astronomy, physics. Lexicons of hieroglyphic, hieratic, demotic Egyptian characters. An antique oil lamp and a modern reproduction Rosetta stone. Where is the logic that can tie all this together? Is it any wonder we all thought he was mad?

"But even a madman must have reasons for what he does. And there may be circumstances in which such a collection would *not* be mad, in which it would be the most effective tool one could use. Suppose, for example, that a man has been dropped into a foreign country with an important mission to perform. Suppose that through some miscalculation or mischance he has arrived without any prior knowledge of that country. Its language, its culture, its history, even the most basic principles of its science are a blank to him. Yet a knowledge of these things is vital to his ability to pass himself off as a native of the place, to move about in it undetected until his mission is complete. What does he do? What *can* he do except try to rectify the situation, by acquiring the basics of the knowledge he so desperately needs? And where can he find this knowledge? In just such books as we saw in the burglar's collection.

"But the burglar has been collecting other things as well. Those lexicons, and that reproduction Rosetta stone. I don't need to remind you of the importance of the Rosetta stone, how its parallel inscriptions in Greek and Egyptian provided the key with which all other Egyptian inscriptions have been unlocked. But have you ever considered how it would have served ancient Egyptian scholars equally well to unlock the secrets of the Greek? And have you ever considered how our own lexicons are Rosetta stones too, because they would have enabled those same Egyptian scholars to unlock the secrets of modern English?"

"What are you saying, Paul? That our burglar is an Egyptian? But modern Egyptians don't use hieroglyphics. You of all people should know that."

"Modern Egyptians don't. But our burglar is *not* a modern Egyptian!

"Dr. Howard, yesterday I told you my theory about the identity of the Carter mummy. You'll recall that you dismissed it very quickly. Maybe you were justified, given the fantastic nature of the claim and the lack of any solid evidence to support it. But as a scientist you must recognize that a thing isn't false simply because it hasn't been proven true. Even if it *appears* to be false in the light of the evidence available today, tomorrow *new* evidence may show the thing in a very different light. Maybe that light hasn't dawned on you yet. Even the most obvious proofs can be overlooked if you don't know what you're searching for, or willfully misinterpreted if you don't like what you find. But there are some proofs so glaring that they *can't* be overlooked, *can't* be mistaken for anything but what they truly are.

"Look at the screen! Do you see that figure sitting there? Do you see how thin and black it is? A geriatric patient? Old age doesn't do that to people. It takes more than a century of living to do that. It takes death and embalming and lying entombed in a burning desert for three thousand years. My God, man, do I have to spell it out for you?

"This is no ordinary burglar! It's the Carter mummy come to life! It's Nyarlathotep himself, risen from the grave of ancient Egypt to revive his evil cult in our modern world!"

Here Paul fell silent, his arguments exhausted. Maybe he had not presented them as calmly as he would have liked. But there were some subjects that could not be discussed calmly. Howard would understand that. But Howard frowned and would not meet his eyes.

"I'm sorry, Paul. When you came to see me yesterday morning, I had no idea how far this had gone. I should have recognized then the strain you've been under. But *you* must recognize it's only the strain that makes you talk as you do, because none of this is true. How *could* it be true? A dead man can't come back after one hour, let alone three thousand years. And this one's embalmed! Brained and gutted! His vital organs sealed in jars! No amount of Egyptian magic can get around that. As for Nyarlathotep and his cult, I tell you again there's nothing to them. The only danger to be feared from them is the danger of you worrying yourself into a breakdown. Forget about them. Forget about the burglar too. We'll catch him soon enough. This tape of yours will be a great help. Meanwhile, why not take the rest of the day off? Better still, take the rest of the week. You'll feel all the better for it on Monday morning."

Paul did not try to argue further. That would only give Howard more cause to doubt his sanity, and he had cause enough already. Yet Paul did not blame Howard for not believing him. Howard had only reacted as any reasonable person would have done when confronted with the same evidence. And in a sense Paul *had* been insane, insane to think he could convince *anyone* of so unbelievable a truth. He knew better now. And he knew something else as

*"Look at the screen! Do you see that figure sitting there? Do you see how thin and black it is? A geriatric patient? Old age doesn't do that to people. It takes more than a century of living to do that. It takes death and embalming and lying entombed in a burning desert for three thousand years."*

well. If only he could recognize the threat this mummy posed to the world, then only he could act to prevent it.

## 6

The mummy lay under electric lights on a shiny metal table. Its unwrapped body had an unfinished look, as if a sculptor had set out to make a man of sticks and mud and given up halfway through. Only the head seemed near complete, and it looked more like an African tribal mask than anything human. Yet none of this was any different from the first time Paul saw the mummy. He was disappointed by this. He had been hoping to find some change, some subtle alteration in position or expression, anything to show that he was not crazy as Howard thought, that what he believed was true. But the mummy gave him nothing. I have kept my secrets for three thousand years, it seemed to say. Why should I reveal them now to you?

"You needn't be so coy," Paul said. "There's nobody to overhear us at this time of night. There's nobody else in this whole wing except at the guard station on the floor above. So we can say what we like without fear of interruption. Maybe you won't understand me, but it doesn't really matter. Sometimes it's a comfort just to hear a human voice, even if it's your own. And sometimes just putting things into words can help to make them clear.

"You see, I know who you are. It wasn't hard to figure out with the trail you left behind you. The pieces of the puzzle were easy to put together. I know who you are and what you've been up to, today and in your previous existence three thousand years ago. I know what purpose brought you to the court of Nephren-Ka. I know how you made the pharaoh your tool to help you accomplish it. I know how, when the tool was broken and the pharaoh was slain, you abandoned your purpose and followed him into death. But death for you was not death as we mortals understand it. It was only waiting. Waiting for a more fertile soil, a more auspicious season, in which to sow your seeds of evil. Waiting for here and now.

"It wasn't a bad plan. The world has changed a lot in the last three thousand years, mostly to your advantage. Your world was a small, insular land under the thumb of a conservative priesthood. My world offers religious freedom and limitless capabilities for global communication. It offers a populace that has rejected the old answers and is eager to be given new ones. What great following could you not acquire in such a place and time? What great works could you not accomplish? You could purify the world with fire and blood. You could even bring back your pre-Egyptian gods.

"But something went wrong, didn't it? Something happened to keep you here, hidden away in the museum basement. Something much bigger than your need to prepare yourself for your strange new life in this strange new world. It was your priests, of course. They may have been wise in some ways, but in others they were pretty ignorant. They didn't know what organs a body needed for a successful resurrection, so they saw no reason to prepare your body different from any other mummy. It must have been a shock to wake up like that, with your vital organs gone, your chest and belly and even your head empty of everything but a few dry herbs. It certainly put a hitch in your plans, because it made it impossible for you to pass yourself off as a man among men. And so you've been hiding here, pretending to be dead by day, by night trying to track down the knowledge you need to undo the damage the embalmers did to you. The knowledge you need to restore yourself completely to life.

"I don't know how long it will take you. I don't even know how long it is since you began. But there's one thing I *do* know. Sooner or later, with all the dark powers at your disposal, you're going to succeed. I can't sit by and let that happen, because I know what it would mean to the future of my civilization. So I've come to put an end to your plans, and you with them.

"First I'll see whether your Egyptian magic can really help you return from death. I'm a scientist, you know, and I can't pass up this unique opportunity to add to mankind's knowledge. And then—"

Here he paused and felt the reassuring weight of the revolver in his lab coat pocket.

"Then I'll see whether my twentieth-century technology can't send you back to death again. Because I'm a human being first."

## 7

What a rotten week *this* was turning out to be, Howard thought next morning as he left his office on his way to the X-ray lab. Two more burglaries in as many nights, and they were still no closer to catching the burglar. For a while the hunt had looked almost promising, with the discovery of the burglar's secret den and the capture of his likeness on Paul O'Neil's videotape. But it was useless to have his likeness if no one could identify it, and it was useless to know his den if he would not return to it. So despite their discoveries they were no better off than before.

As a matter of fact they were worse off, considering what his obsession with the mystery had done to Paul. Howard was seriously worried about that young man. He had been worried two days ago, when Paul first came to him with his wild theories about Nyarlathotep and the Carter mummy. He had been more worried yesterday, when it became all too obvious that the young man's obsession was getting dangerously out of hand. But it could hardly have gone otherwise once he started meddling with the deadly poison of occultism. Maybe it was partly Howard's fault for not warning him against it more openly. But Paul might have questioned how he knew, and Howard had no desire to resurrect his youthful indiscretion at this late date, or the less than innocent part it had played in the death of poor Bertrand.

Besides, he had still hoped that Paul was only feeling the strain of overwork, and that a little rest was all he needed to recover. But that hope was looking pretty foolish in the light of this morning's revelation. For Paul had disappeared. His wife had telephoned twice already, looking for him. She said he had left the house last night, claiming to have some late work to do at the museum. She said he had never returned. Howard did not know about any late work, but the guard station records showed that Paul *had* come back last night around ten, and that he had left again an hour later. Howard could only advise Mrs. O'Neil to call the police. Yet he made up his mind that, when she *did* find her husband, he would urge her to place him under psychiatric care.

But now he had still another problem to deal with. The white-coated X-ray technician was waiting for him at the lab door.

"Here I am," Howard said. "What have you got to show me? You said on the telephone that our burglar had struck again."

"It looks that way," the technician answered as he ushered Howard into the lab. "This morning I took some new exposures of the Carter mummy's head, to replace the fogged ones from the other day. After I finished developing them, I hung them up beside the old ones to compare the results. I found—But see for yourself."

Howard studied the ghostly images floating before the florescent screen. It did not take long for even his untrained eyes to recognize the differences between them.

"It can't be!"

"That's just what I said when *I* saw it. But it obviously is. The shapes of the two skulls are completely different. There's no getting around the fact that this isn't the same mummy."

But Howard seemed not to hear him. "You fool!" he said softly. "You poor, damned fool!" Then he took two steps backward and collapsed into a waiting chair.

"Dr. Howard, are you ill? Is there anything I can do?"

"Yes. Call the police. Have them send somebody out here right away. Tell them—tell them Paul O'Neil has run off with a valuable mummy. Tell them he's insane and probably dangerous. Maybe *they* can stop him. Then tell them to call his wife and arrange to get hold of his dental records."

"Paul O'Neil? Dental records?"

"Yes, man! Are you blind? Look at the plates! Since when do ancient Egyptian mummies have modern fillings in their teeth?"

Lisa looked up from her drink to see a young man standing on the opposite side of her table. He was tall, slender and good looking in a quiet, intellectual way. His features were open and friendly. His Miskatonic University tee shirt was his one concession to the club. Except for this, he looked as much out of place here as Lisa herself.

He pulled out the chair and sat down. "I was supposed to meet some friends here tonight, but they're running a little late. Then I saw you sitting by yourself, and I thought you looked like you could use some company. My name's Aaron."

"Mine's Lisa."

"You're not one of the regulars, are you, Lisa?"

"Does it show? No, I'm not a Goth, if that's what you're asking. I've never been here before. I probably wouldn't be here now, except that a friend of mine made me come. She thought it would be good for me, or something."

"And has it been? Good for you, I mean."

"Not so you'd notice. But it's probably my own fault. I knew it was a bad idea when my friend suggested it. But when she promised to show me around and introduce me to some kindred spirits, I hoped it would be okay. But my friend disappeared soon after we arrived, paired off with some vampire wannabe for a few hours of mutual bloodletting. Fortunately, I brought my own car. But now I don't know whether I'm supposed to wait for her or leave her to find her own way home."

"I can see how that would be annoying."

"And that's not the half of it. There's also the little matter of the kindred spirits I was supposed to meet. That's the part I found *really* depressing."

"Oh? Why is that?"

"Do you have to ask?" Lisa waved her hand around the room. "Just look at them! Clothes black, as if they just got back from Queen Victoria's funeral. Hair dyed black too. I know, because I saw the roots growing out. Faces white from staying out of the sun, or at least painted to look that way. And the expressions on those faces! I swear, they must spend hours in front of a mirror to get that perfect blend of pained intensity and melancholy boredom. But none of it's *real.* It's all playacting and make-believe. Underneath it all they're just ordinary people like you and me, just ordinary people trying to forget how ordinary they are."

"I'm not saying you're wrong," said Aaron, smiling. "But after all, what did you expect?"

"Expect?" The question surprised her. Until that moment she had not been aware that she had expected anything. And yet—

"You're right. I guess I *was* expecting something, something a little deeper than a Byronic pose. I was hoping that the pose had a meaning, that it was the outward reflection of something inward and very real. That's it. I was hoping to find people who were a little more real than the rest of us. People who knew a thing or two about life, and who faced up to it anyway without flinching. People who celebrated darkness because the world is dark and they were at home in it—"

Here she broke off, suddenly embarrassed by the sense of her own words.

"God! Where did *that* come from? I hope it's the wine talking. I'd hate to think that underneath it all I'm just like the rest of them."

"Not like them," said Aaron. "Not many of them would have the brains to recognize that there might be something bigger than themselves, or the heart to try to find it. These people are playing at being something they're not. This club is where they come to play. But they aren't the only people, and this isn't the only club. Listen. Our friends have stood us up. Why not let me take you someplace and show you something a little more *real?* That is, if you're interested."

Lisa hesitated. She had not come here to be picked up. Still, the evening so far had been a total bust, and this was the first promising offer she had had.

"I'm interested," she said. "When do we start?"

## 2

Twenty minutes later, Lisa drove her car at Aaron's direction into the old industrial district, between blocks of dead factories and empty warehouses that industry had abandoned. The buildings loomed like tall black cliffs over the half-lit streets. The upper windows were blind and dark, the lower ones bricked up as if to repel a siege. The walls were defaced with torn bills and spray-painted slogans. It was almost a shock to find cars in such a place. But there they were, parked along both sides of the street in ever increasing numbers.

"Park where you can," said Aaron. "We won't get much closer than this."

Lisa pulled into a space between a new BMW and an old VW Beetle. But it was not until they had gotten out of the car and walked awhile that Lisa saw the people. They were standing in line along the sidewalk under the brick wall of a warehouse. They were mostly the same Gothic types that they had left behind at the first club, with the same white faces starkly offset by the same black hair and clothes. But their expressions of melancholy indifference were starting to crack under the strain of waiting in line. Some of them stared at Aaron and Lisa resentfully as they passed.

"The line looks pretty long," said Lisa. "Do you think we'll get in?"

"Don't worry. I know the management."

This was no empty boast apparently. He did no more than exchange a look with the bearded giant of a doorman before the latter unhooked the chain to let him pass, drawing a murmur of protest from those in line. The doorman almost re-hooked the chain before Lisa could follow, but Aaron stopped him. "She's with me," he said. The doorman shrugged and let her pass too.

Inside looked more like a theater than a dance club. The building was only a shell anyway, a converted warehouse easily large enough to have served as a hangar for a blimp. The third nearest the entrance was crowded with tables and chairs, with people sitting at or milling around them. But the center, where one would have expected to find a dance floor, was occupied instead by a sort of stage, a stepped platform maybe thirty feet wide by three tall with a black curtain hanging across the front.

Even the lighting had a theatrical look. The area between the entrance and the stage was an island of light in the midst of a sea of darkness. The area to either side of the stage, and behind it as much as could be seen over the curtain, was black. The invisible ceiling hung over everything like the night sky, with banks of lights shining down from the unseen rafters like so many moons and stars. The lower hall murmured with many voices, while somewhere in the darkness overhead the recorded voice of a female vocalist sang of the darkness gathering in her soul.

Aaron led Lisa to one of the few unoccupied tables, not far from the entrance and even less from the broad aisle that ran between the entrance and the stage. They sat down, and she looked around at the people sitting at the neighboring tables. In appearance they were not much different from the Goths in the line outside. Maybe they were a little more conservatively dressed, with contemporary dark clothes and glasses standing in for the more usual Victorian costume, but that was all.

Yet there *was* a difference, and it was not long before Lisa realized what it was. The typical Gothic air of spiritual torment and melancholy boredom was largely absent here. In its place was a most un-Gothic air of barely suppressed hilarity and eager anticipation. Lisa thought that this was probably the effect of alcohol or cocaine. There did not appear to be much consumption of either going on, but that did not mean that the attendees had not indulged themselves before coming.

Besides the people sitting at the tables, there were several others in long black robes circulating between them. Lisa assumed that they were servers taking orders until one of them approached their own table and held out an open coffee can. Her appearance was startling even here. Her face was thin and very pale, with dark circles under her staring eyes. Her graying hair appeared to have been bobbed with a dull kitchen knife. But the startling part was that none of this appeared to be makeup. Lisa wondered how such a person had managed to get past the doorman. She was genuinely surprised when Aaron asked:

"How much money do you have?"

"About twenty dollars. Why?"

"Give me ten. For the upkeep of the temple."

"The temple? I don't understand."

"I'll explain later."

She gave him the money and he dropped it in the can. After the robed woman moved on to the next table, she turned to him to ask for her explanation. But just then the recorded song was cut off in mid-lyric. The lights dimmed almost to darkness. The murmur of voices fell into a hush as everyone's attention was turned on the curtained stage.

## 3

The performance began with all the excitement of a high school pageant. Two black figures converged in silence on the stage from opposite sides of the hall. They walked slowly through the darkness in moving circles of light, in long black robes and pointed hoods that covered their forms and faces. They mounted the steps at the center of the stage, then went off again to left and right, drawing the two halves of the curtain behind them. But the stage thus revealed was no less dark than the curtain that had concealed it.

When the curtain was fully drawn, the figures returned to stand side by side at the front of the stage. They pushed back their hoods to uncover the heads of a man and woman so like in appearance that they must have been brother and sister. They were young, blond and attractive. They wore thin silver circlets on their brows. They looked impassively over the audience to the back of the darkened hall.

Several members of the audience turned in their seats to look in the same direction. Lisa turned too, and saw that a third figure was standing in another circle of light at the end of the aisle. This figure was robed and hooded like the others, but in blood red rather than black. Now it began to walk toward the stage at a slow and measured pace. Over the loudspeaker a male voice intoned:

*From the darkness of N'kai,*
*From the shadows of K'n-yan,*
*From the caverns of the earth,*
    *Arise to us, O Buried One!*

The man and woman met the third figure at the top of the steps. There it stopped between them and turned back to face the hall. It pushed back its hood as the others had done, to uncover the head of another woman. But where the first was fair and impassive, this one was dark with an excited, even exalted expression lighting her youthful face. On her head was a tall golden tiara.

Slowly, solemnly, she removed the tiara from her head and placed it in the hands of the first woman, who in turn placed it gently on the floor. She took off her robe and passed it to the man, who folded it and laid it down likewise. Nude, she turned her back on the hall, and all three began to walk toward the center of the stage. The voice over the loudspeaker continued:

*Taking matter from the dark,*
*Taking contour from the light,*
*Taking body in the stone,*
*Appear to us, O Hidden One!*

The light traveled with them to the center of the stage, where it now discovered two black posts standing together about five feet high and the same distance apart. The nude woman stopped between the posts and raised her hands to touch them on either side of her, while the others tied her wrists to waiting rings. When she was securely bound, the man lifted the dark cascade of her waist-long hair, and the woman produced a pair of scissors and began to cut it off above the shoulders.

Lisa stirred uneasily in her chair, increasingly uncomfortable with the way this was going. She had heard of things like spanking clubs, but she had never dreamed of setting foot in one. She was embarrassed to be here. She was disappointed to learn that this was Aaron's idea of something real. She was insulted to think that he had imagined that it would be her idea too. She got up to leave, but Aaron caught her by the arm.

"What is it?" he asked her.

"I'm not into this scene. I want to go."

"But you can't go now. The ceremony has begun. Sit down. Everyone's looking at you."

This last was at least partly true. The people around her were glaring at her in annoyance. She sat down again, and Aaron released her arm. The voice over the loudspeaker continued:

*The depth of Thine imponderable wisdom,*
*The height of Thine illimitable power,*
*The fire of Thine insatiable lust,*
*Impart to us, O Generous One!*

The man and woman each took up a thin black rod about two feet long, and began—

But no! Maybe Aaron could prevent her from leaving, but he could not force her to witness this degrading spectacle. She closed her eyes against the sight. But she could not close her ears against the sound, the slow, deliberate sound of cutting blows on naked flesh, counting off the seconds like a metronome in hell.

But this was not the only sound. Somewhere in the audience a single voice accompanied the blows with a shouted word or phrase. Soon other voices took up the phrase and repeated it in unison, until it was loud enough to cover up even the sound of the blows.

What was it they were shouting? It was not an English phrase, or a Spanish phrase, or a phrase in any language that Lisa could recognize. It seemed to be a single barbaric name repeated over and over. But the shout had grown to a ringing thunder before she could make out what it was.

*Tsathoggua!*
*Tsathoggua!*
*Tsathoggua!*

Then all at once the voices and the blows fell silent. Lisa opened her eyes.

The beating at least was over. The beaters had laid down their rods and covered their heads and were backing away from the bound woman in a grotesque crouching posture. But the effects of the beating were plain to see in the body of its victim. She hung between the posts as if dead, her knees slightly bent, her head bowed below the level of her shoulders. Her back was crisscrossed from shoulders to thighs with the marks of her punishment.

Yet all this was of secondary interest. For the stage itself had changed dramatically while Lisa's eyes were closed. The circle of light had grown wider, pushing outward from the center of the stage to illumine something at the back. This was a statue in dull black stone set on a raised dais. Even without the dais it would have been as tall as a man. But the man would have been standing at his full height, while the statue was hunkered down in the posture of a toad. It was in fact the statue of a toad. Its wide mouth was calm and impassive, its round eyes closed in sleep. Only its face was fully lit. The rest of it seemed half dissolved in the darkness behind the stage.

Now, slowly, painfully, the bound woman came to life again. She raised her head to look at the statue before her, and turned up her palms in a gesture of acquiescence. The voice over the loudspeaker intoned:

*This our offering of flesh,*
*This our sacrifice of blood,*
*This our hecatomb of pain,*
*Accept of us, O Hungry One!*

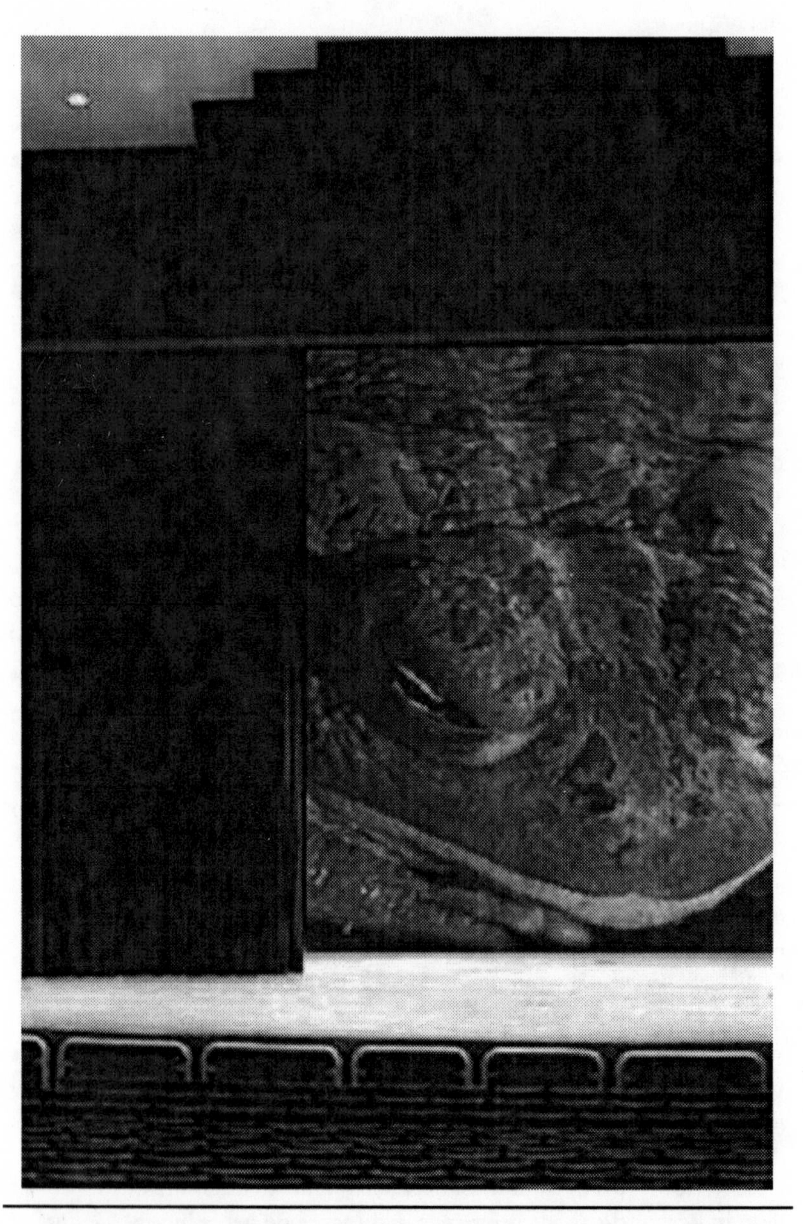

*Even without the dais it would have been as tall as a man. But the man would have been standing at his full height, while the statue was hunkered down in the posture of a toad. It was in fact the statue of a toad. Its wide mouth was calm and impassive, its round eyes closed in sleep. Only its face was fully lit. The rest of it seemed half dissolved in the darkness behind the stage.*

For a moment nothing happened. Then the eyes in the stone face opened into luminous slits like crescent moons. The wide mouth opened too, and a long pale tongue came whipping out to curl itself around the waist of the bound woman, who began to throw herself from side to side against her bonds and scream uncontrollably.

4

Lisa did not see what happened next. Her overturned chair crashed to the floor behind her, and Aaron's voice called after her in a sort of whispered shout. But she did not stop, because she did not hear them. She could not hear anything while that mad screaming was going on. She could not stop while that terrible rite was still in progress.

Outside, the sidewalk was mercifully empty. The people in line must have all given up and gone home. There was no one to pry into her distress, no one to torment her with questions she could not answer. She collapsed gasping and sobbing against the reassuringly solid brick wall.

She was still in this position when she heard footsteps approach and stop before her, and a low voice speak her name. She looked up to see Aaron, as she had known she would. But his voice had sounded tense and strange, and his face looked very pale in the lamplight.

Embarrassed, she made an effort to pull herself together. "I must look like a perfect idiot," she said, wiping her eyes. "I don't know what came over me. I don't know why I was so frightened. You'd think I'd never seen a horror show before!"

Then she added, almost pleadingly, "That's all it was, right? A show?"

He did not answer for some time, though more than once he seemed on the point of doing so. When he spoke again, the strangeness in his voice was almost gone.

"Of course it was a show! What else *could* it have been? Anyway, it's over now. Come on. I'll walk you to your car."

THE TALES OF INSPECTOR LEGRASSE
H. P. LOVECRAFT & C. J. HENDERSON

AVAILABLE TO ORDER

WALTER C. DEBILL, JR.

THE BLACK SUTRA

AVAILABLE TO ORDER

AVAILABLE TO ORDER

OMENS
Richard Gavin